SHERLOCK HOLMES

and the Adventure of the Three Garridebs

Based on the stories of
Sir Arthur Conan Doyle

Adapted by **Murray Shaw** and **M. J. Cosson**
Illustrated by **Sophie Rohrbach** and **JT Morrow**

GRAPHIC UNIVERSE™ • MINNEAPOLIS • NEW YORK

Grateful acknowledgment to Dame Jean Conan Doyle for permission to use the Sherlock Holmes characters created by Sir Arthur Conan Doyle

Graphic Universe™
A division of Lerner Publishing Group, Inc.
241 First Avenue North
Minneapolis, MN 55401 U.S.A.

Website address: www.lernerbooks.com

Shaw, Murray.
    Sherlock Holmes and the adventure of the three Garridebs / based on the stories of Sir Arthur Conan Doyle ; adapted by Murray Shaw and M.J. Cosson ; illustrated by Sophie Rohrbach and J.T. Morrow.
       p   cm. — (On the case with Holmes and Watson ; #13)
    Summary: Retold in graphic novel form, Sherlock Holmes investigates a man who claims that he will have a large inheritance if two more men who share his surname are found. Includes a section explaining Holmes's reasoning and the clues he used to solve the mystery.
       ISBN: 978-0-7613-7091-8 (lib. bdg. : alk. paper)
       I. Graphic novels. (I. Graphic novels. 2. Doyle, Arthur Conan, Sir, 1859-1930. Adventure of the three Garridebs—Adaptations. 3. Mystery and detective stories.) I. Cosson, M. J. II. Rohrbach, Sophie, ill. III. Morrow, J .T., ill. IV. Doyle, Arthur Conan, Sir, 1859-1930. Adventure of the three Garridebs. V. Title.
    PZ7.7.S46Sio 2012
    741.5'973—dc2   2011005114

Manufactured in the United States of America
1—BC—12/31/11

The Story of
SHERLOCK HOLMES
the Famous Detective

Sherlock Holmes and his helpful friend Dr. John Watson are fictional characters created by British writer Sir Arthur Conan Doyle. Doyle published his first novel about the pair, *A Study in Scarlet*, in 1887, and it became very successful. Doyle went on to write fifty-six short stories, as well as three more novels about Holmes's adventures—*The Sign of Four* (1890), *The Hound of the Baskervilles* (1902), and *The Valley of Fear* (1915).

Sherlock Holmes and Dr. Watson have become some of the most famous book characters of all time. Holmes spent most of his time solving mysteries, but he also had a wide array of hobbies, such as playing the violin, boxing, and sword fighting. Watson, a retired army doctor, met Holmes through a mutual friend when Holmes was looking for a roommate. Watson lived with Holmes for several years at 221B Baker Street before marrying and moving out. However, after his marriage, Watson continued to assist Holmes with his cases.

The original versions of the Sherlock Holmes stories are still printed, and many have been made into movies and television shows. Readers continue to be impressed by Holmes's detective methods of observation and scientific reason.

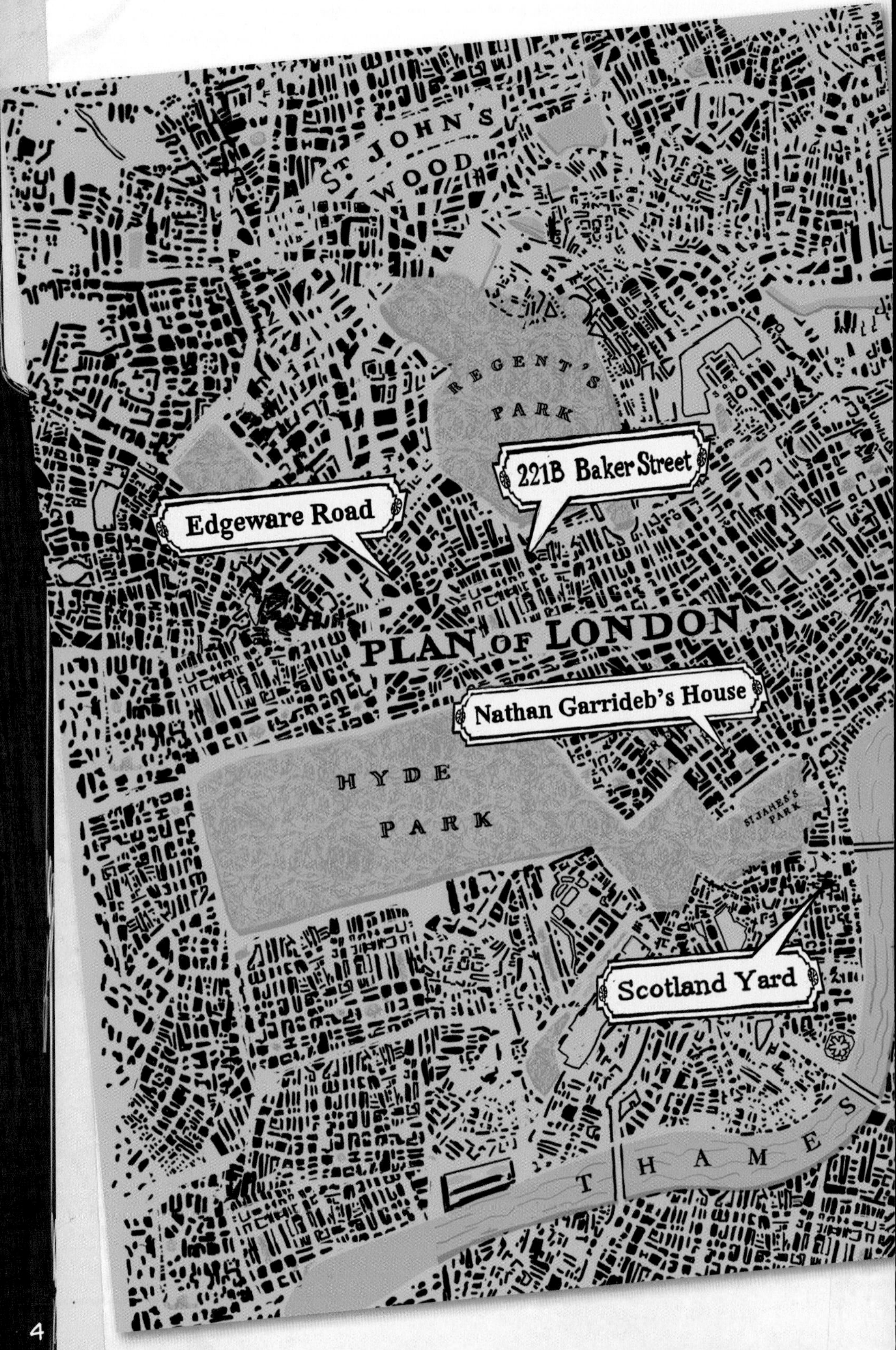
ST. JOHN'S WOOD
REGENT'S PARK
221B Baker Street
Edgeware Road
PLAN OF LONDON
Nathan Garrideb's House
HYDE PARK
ST JAMES'S PARK
Scotland Yard
THAMES

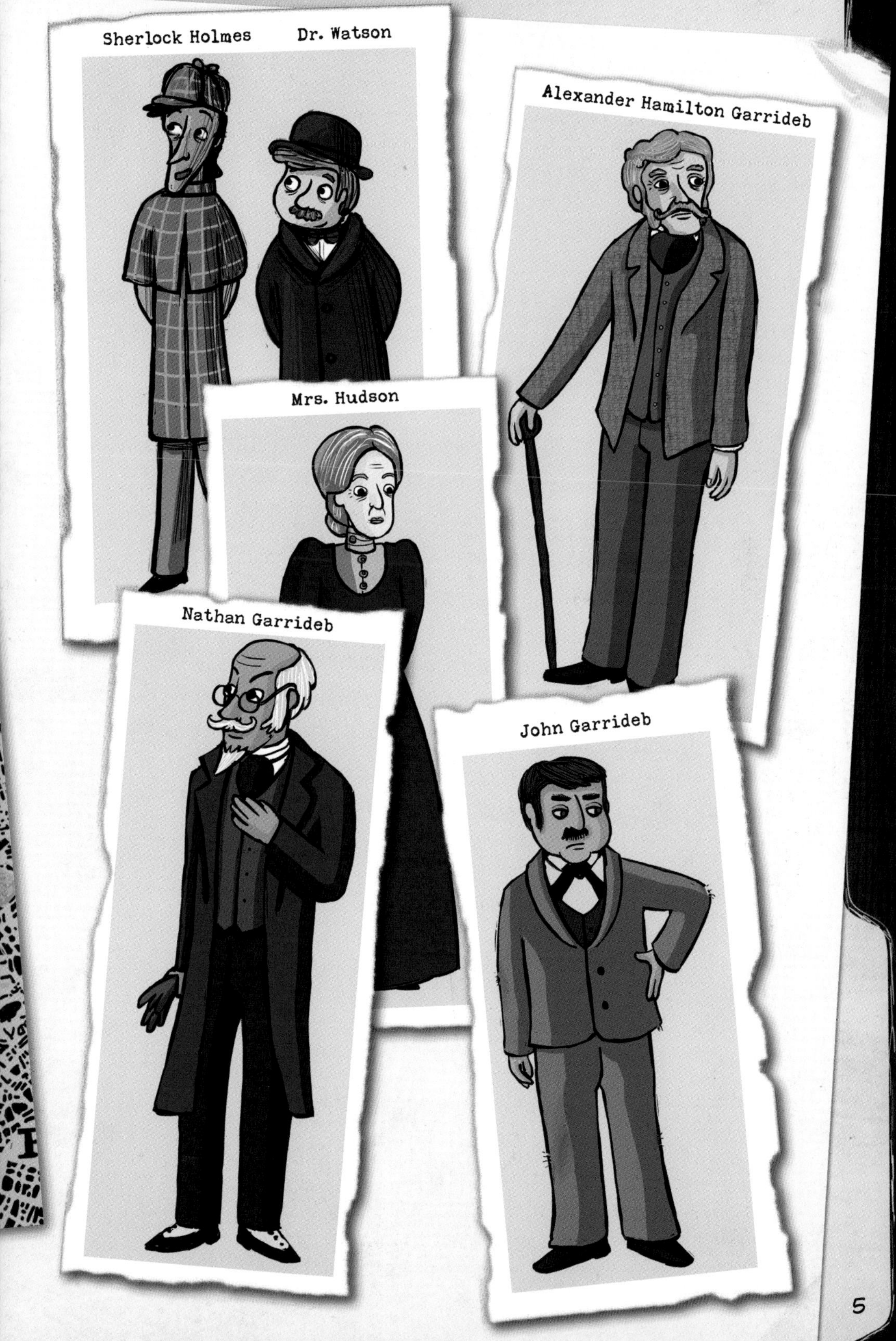
Sherlock Holmes
Dr. Watson
Alexander Hamilton Garrideb
Mrs. Hudson
Nathan Garrideb
John Garrideb

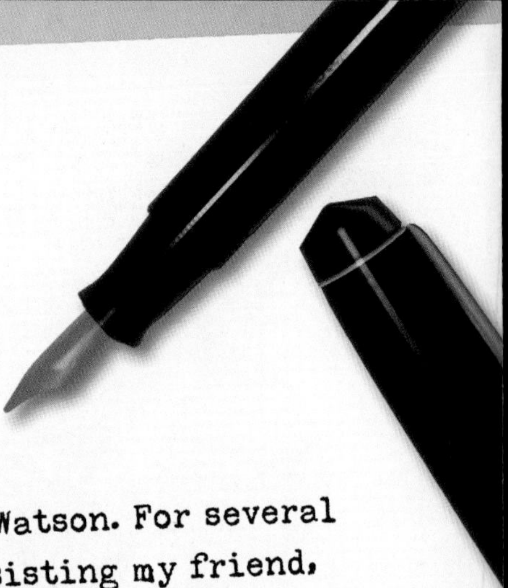

From the Desk of John H. Watson, M.D.

My name is Dr. John H. Watson. For several years, I have been assisting my friend, Sherlock Holmes, in solving mysteries throughout the bustling city of London and beyond. Holmes is a peculiar man—always questioning and reasoning his way through various problems. But when I first met him in 1878, I was immediately intrigued by his oddities.

Holmes has always been more daring than I, and his logical deduction never ceases to amaze me. I have begun writing down all of the adventures I have with Holmes. This is one of those stories.

Sincerely,

Dr. Watson

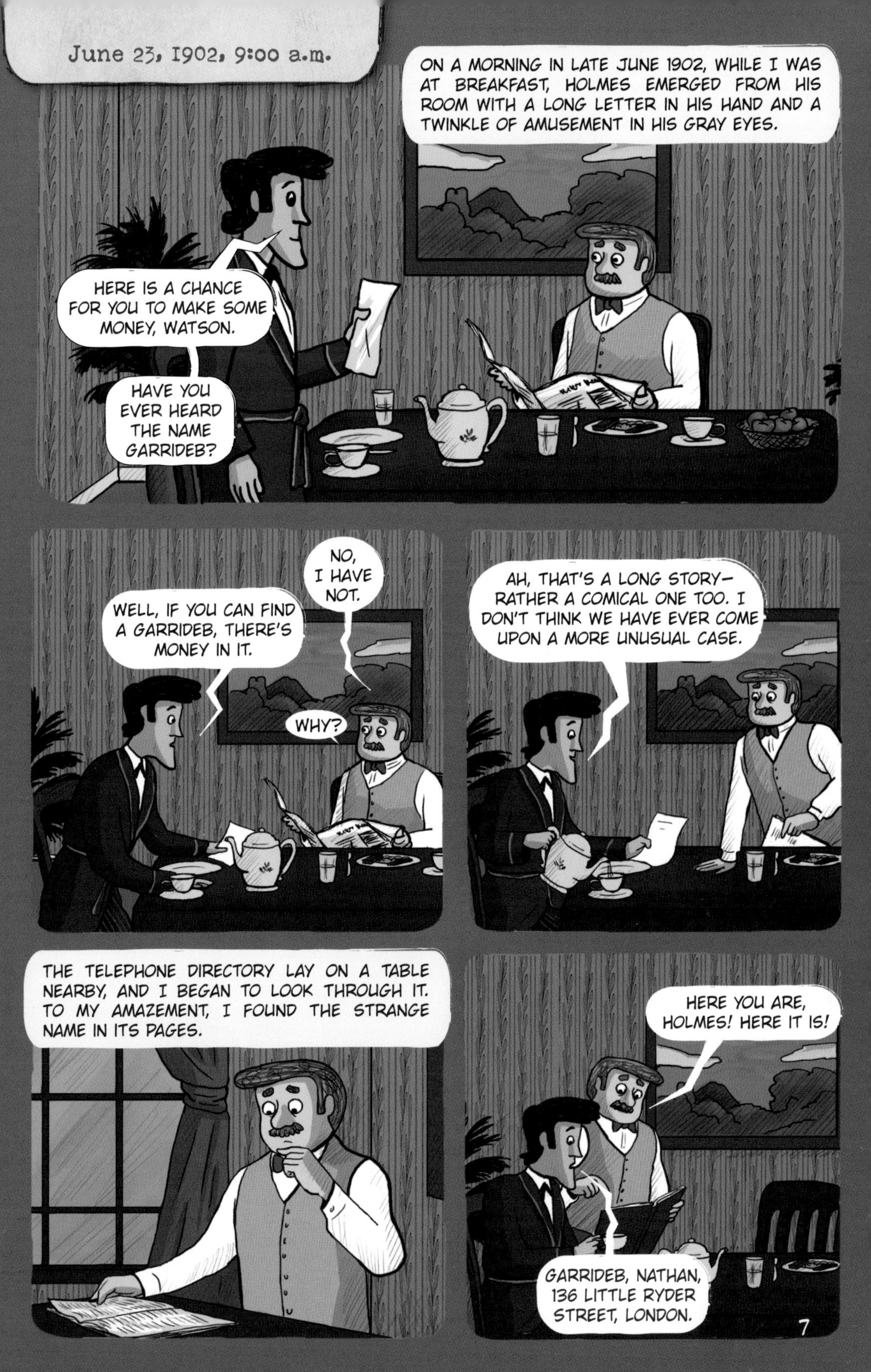
June 23, 1902, 9:00 a.m.
ON A MORNING IN LATE JUNE 1902, WHILE I WAS AT BREAKFAST, HOLMES EMERGED FROM HIS ROOM WITH A LONG LETTER IN HIS HAND AND A TWINKLE OF AMUSEMENT IN HIS GRAY EYES.
HERE IS A CHANCE FOR YOU TO MAKE SOME MONEY, WATSON.
HAVE YOU EVER HEARD THE NAME GARRIDEB?
NO, I HAVE NOT.
WELL, IF YOU CAN FIND A GARRIDEB, THERE'S MONEY IN IT.
WHY?
AH, THAT'S A LONG STORY— RATHER A COMICAL ONE TOO. I DON'T THINK WE HAVE EVER COME UPON A MORE UNUSUAL CASE.
THE TELEPHONE DIRECTORY LAY ON A TABLE NEARBY, AND I BEGAN TO LOOK THROUGH IT. TO MY AMAZEMENT, I FOUND THE STRANGE NAME IN ITS PAGES.
HERE YOU ARE, HOLMES! HERE IT IS!
GARRIDEB, NATHAN, 136 LITTLE RYDER STREET, LONDON.

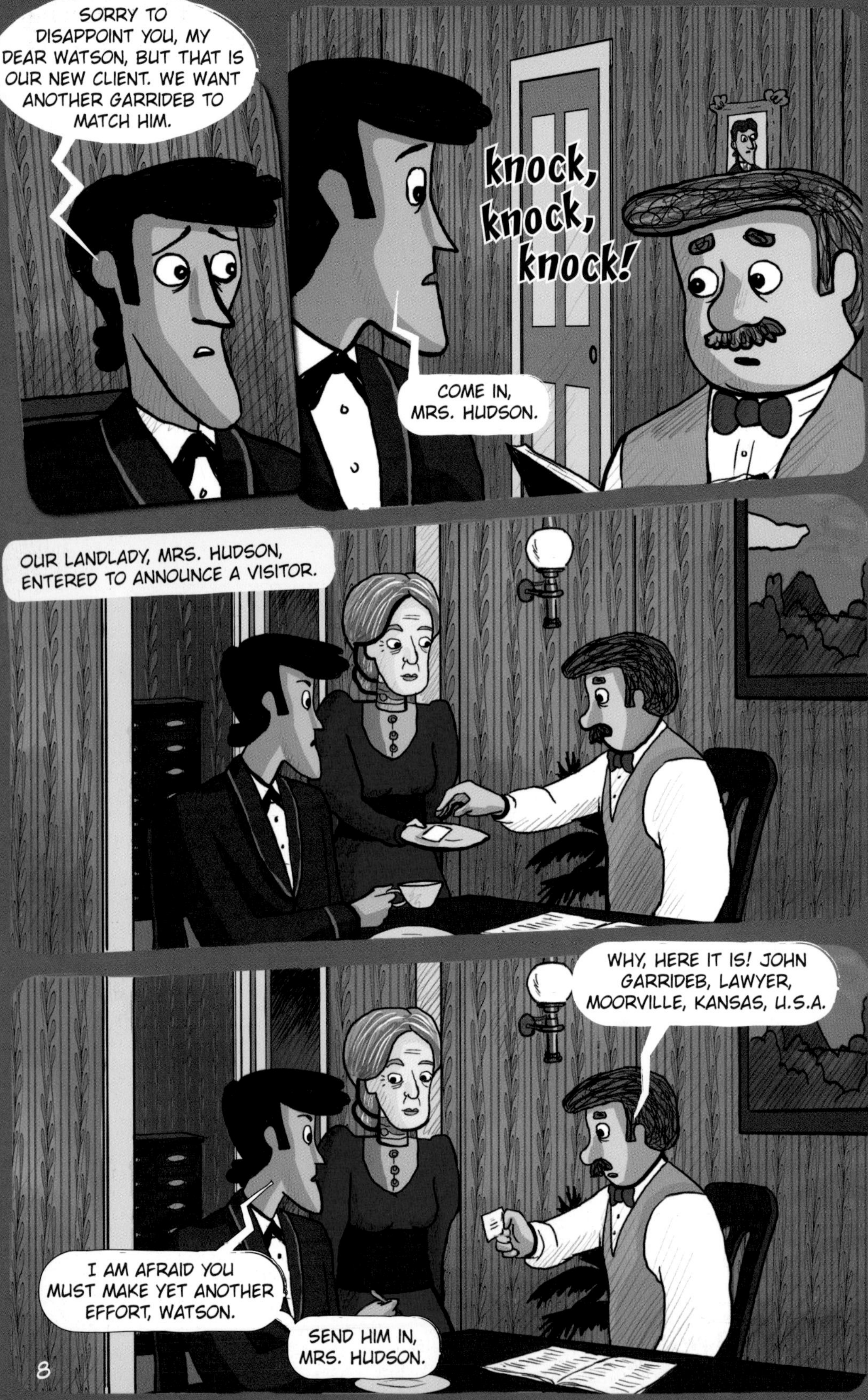
SORRY TO DISAPPOINT YOU, MY DEAR WATSON, BUT THAT IS OUR NEW CLIENT. WE WANT ANOTHER GARRIDEB TO MATCH HIM.
knock, knock, knock!
COME IN, MRS. HUDSON.
OUR LANDLADY, MRS. HUDSON, ENTERED TO ANNOUNCE A VISITOR.
WHY, HERE IT IS! JOHN GARRIDEB, LAWYER, MOORVILLE, KANSAS, U.S.A.
I AM AFRAID YOU MUST MAKE YET ANOTHER EFFORT, WATSON.
SEND HIM IN, MRS. HUDSON.

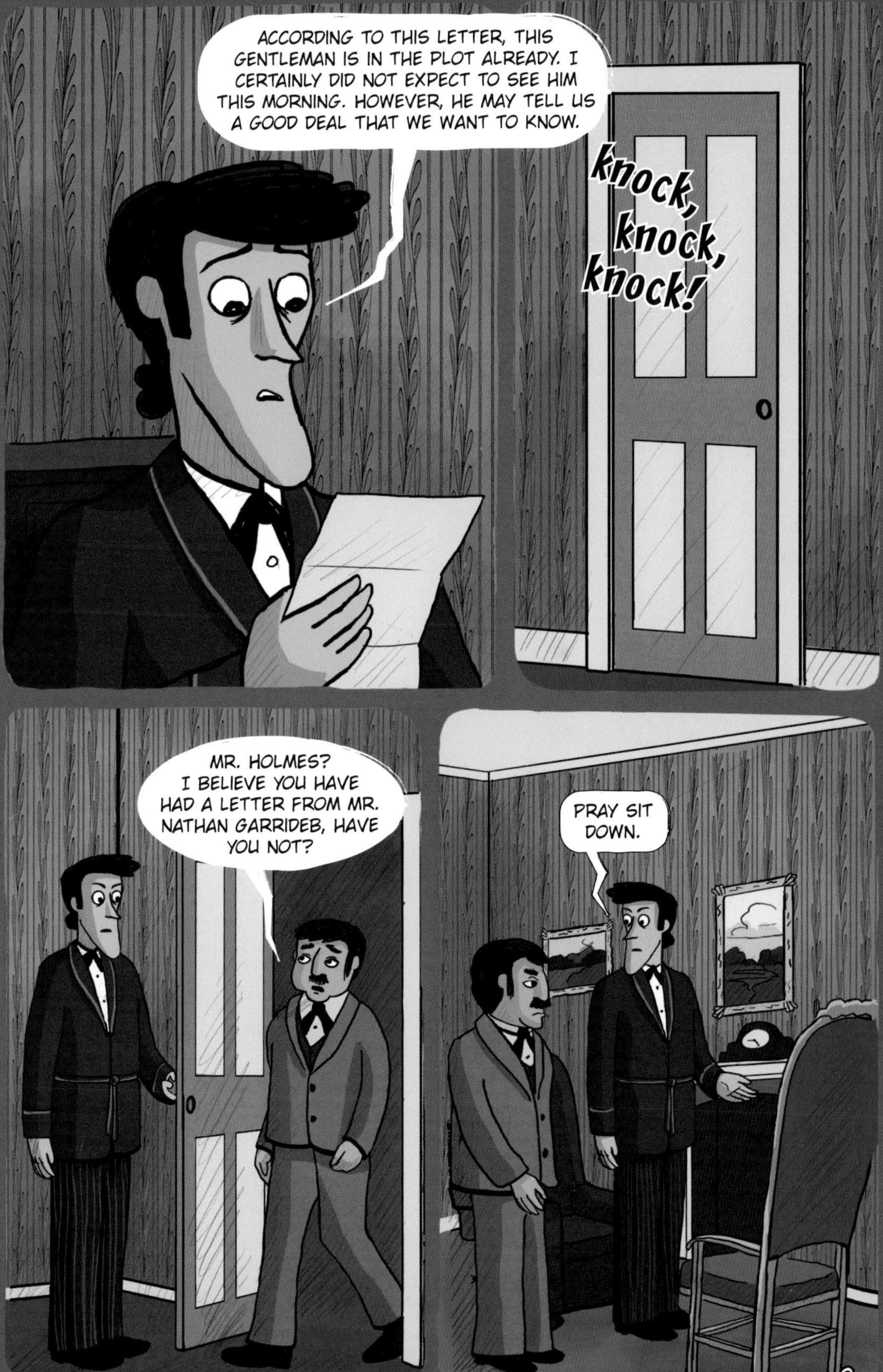
ACCORDING TO THIS LETTER, THIS GENTLEMAN IS IN THE PLOT ALREADY. I CERTAINLY DID NOT EXPECT TO SEE HIM THIS MORNING. HOWEVER, HE MAY TELL US A GOOD DEAL THAT WE WANT TO KNOW.
knock, knock, knock!
MR. HOLMES? I BELIEVE YOU HAVE HAD A LETTER FROM MR. NATHAN GARRIDEB, HAVE YOU NOT?
PRAY SIT DOWN.

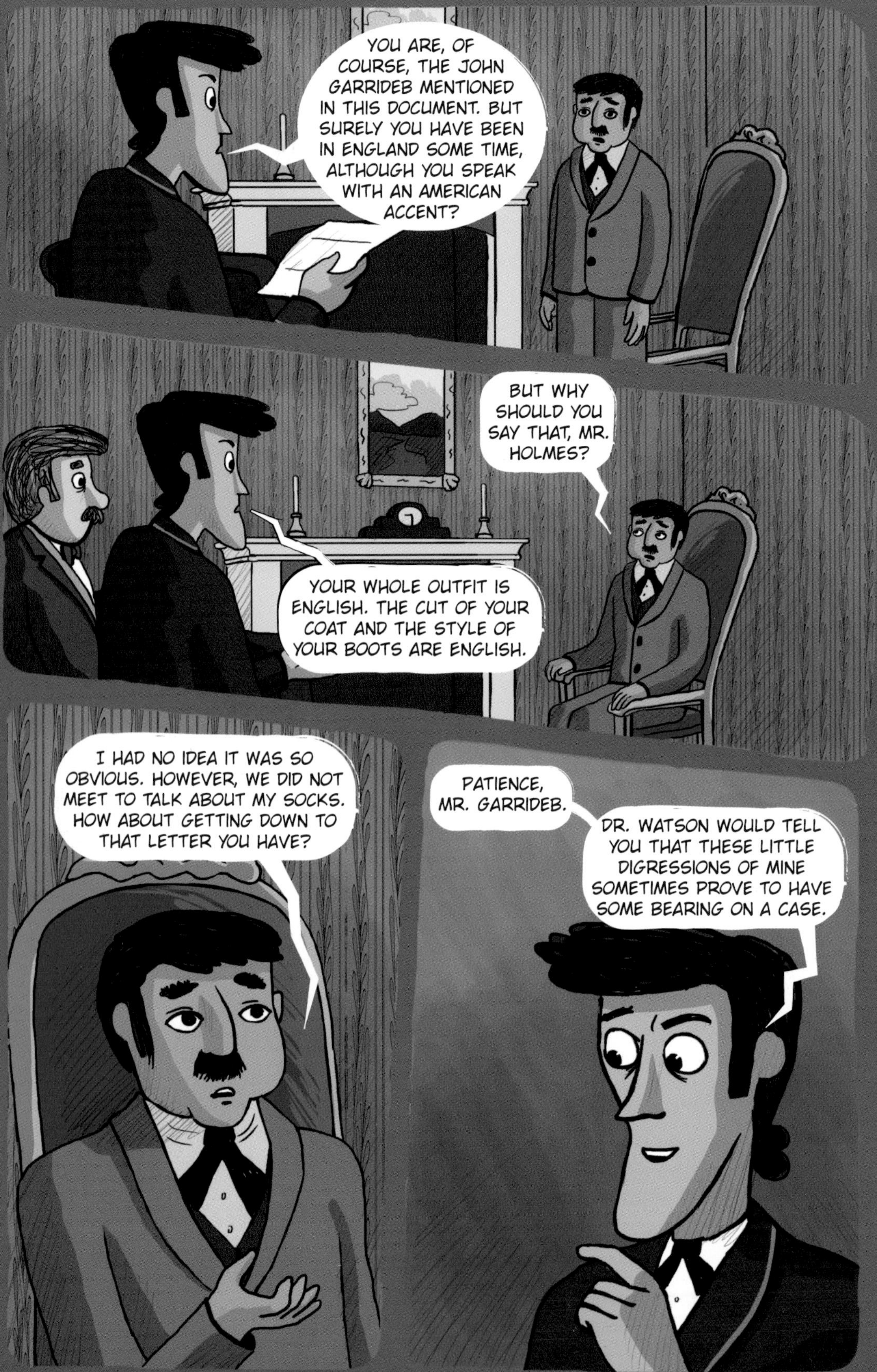
YOU ARE, OF COURSE, THE JOHN GARRIDEB MENTIONED IN THIS DOCUMENT. BUT SURELY YOU HAVE BEEN IN ENGLAND SOME TIME, ALTHOUGH YOU SPEAK WITH AN AMERICAN ACCENT?
BUT WHY SHOULD YOU SAY THAT, MR. HOLMES?
YOUR WHOLE OUTFIT IS ENGLISH. THE CUT OF YOUR COAT AND THE STYLE OF YOUR BOOTS ARE ENGLISH.
I HAD NO IDEA IT WAS SO OBVIOUS. HOWEVER, WE DID NOT MEET TO TALK ABOUT MY SOCKS. HOW ABOUT GETTING DOWN TO THAT LETTER YOU HAVE?
PATIENCE, MR. GARRIDEB.
DR. WATSON WOULD TELL YOU THAT THESE LITTLE DIGRESSIONS OF MINE SOMETIMES PROVE TO HAVE SOME BEARING ON A CASE.

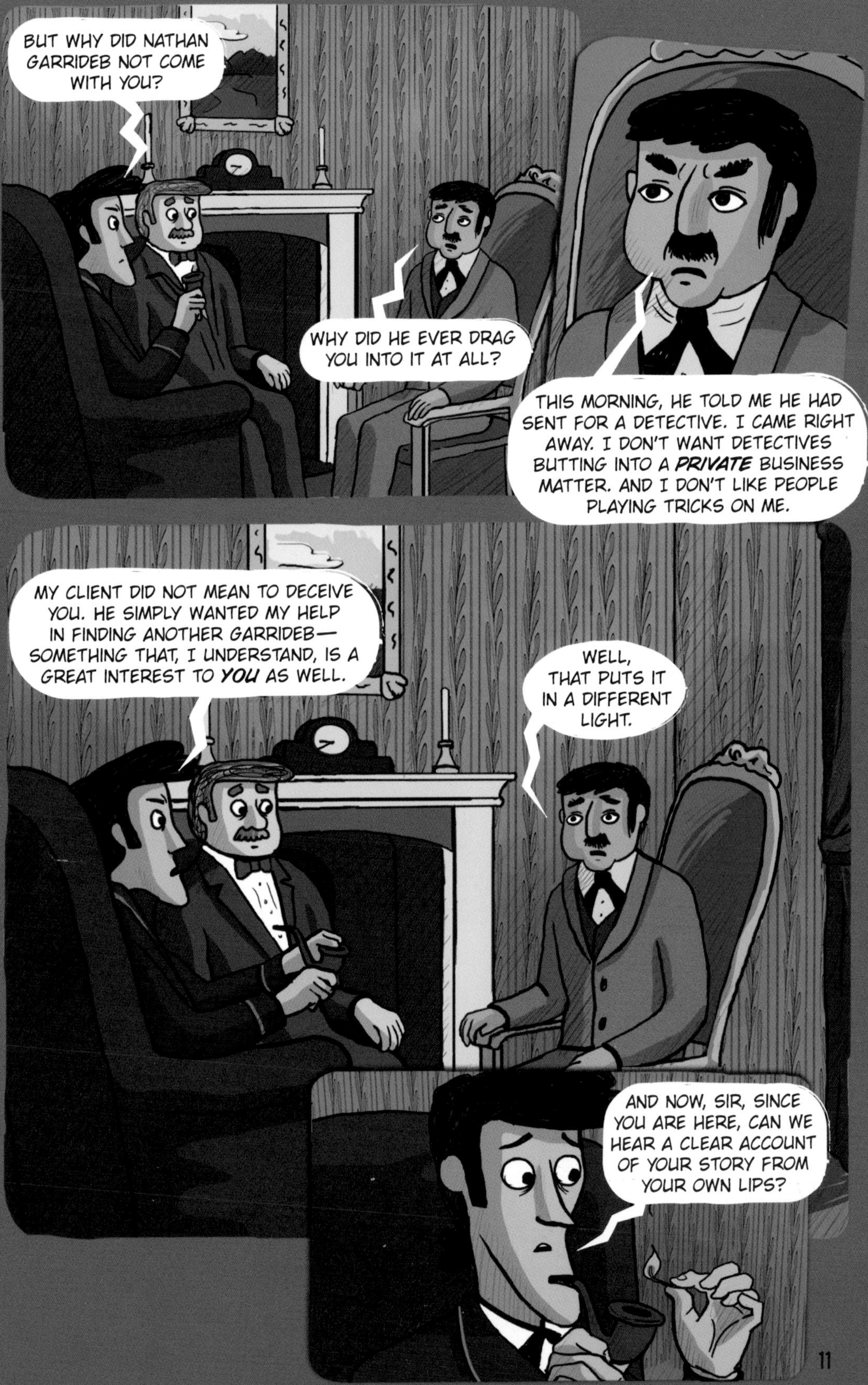
BUT WHY DID NATHAN GARRIDEB NOT COME WITH YOU?
WHY DID HE EVER DRAG YOU INTO IT AT ALL?
THIS MORNING, HE TOLD ME HE HAD SENT FOR A DETECTIVE. I CAME RIGHT AWAY. I DON'T WANT DETECTIVES BUTTING INTO A *PRIVATE* BUSINESS MATTER. AND I DON'T LIKE PEOPLE PLAYING TRICKS ON ME.
MY CLIENT DID NOT MEAN TO DECEIVE YOU. HE SIMPLY WANTED MY HELP IN FINDING ANOTHER GARRIDEB—SOMETHING THAT, I UNDERSTAND, IS A GREAT INTEREST TO *YOU* AS WELL.
WELL, THAT PUTS IT IN A DIFFERENT LIGHT.
AND NOW, SIR, SINCE YOU ARE HERE, CAN WE HEAR A CLEAR ACCOUNT OF YOUR STORY FROM YOUR OWN LIPS?

John Garrideb began by explaining that if Holmes and I were from Kansas, he would not need to explain to us who Alexander Hamilton Garrideb was. That Garrideb made his money in real estate and owned thousands of acres. He had no relatives or children, yet he wanted to leave his fortune to a Garrideb. That was what brought him to seek out John Garrideb, who was working in Topeka, Kansas, when the old gentleman visited. Alexander Hamilton Garrideb was tickled to death to meet another man with his last name.

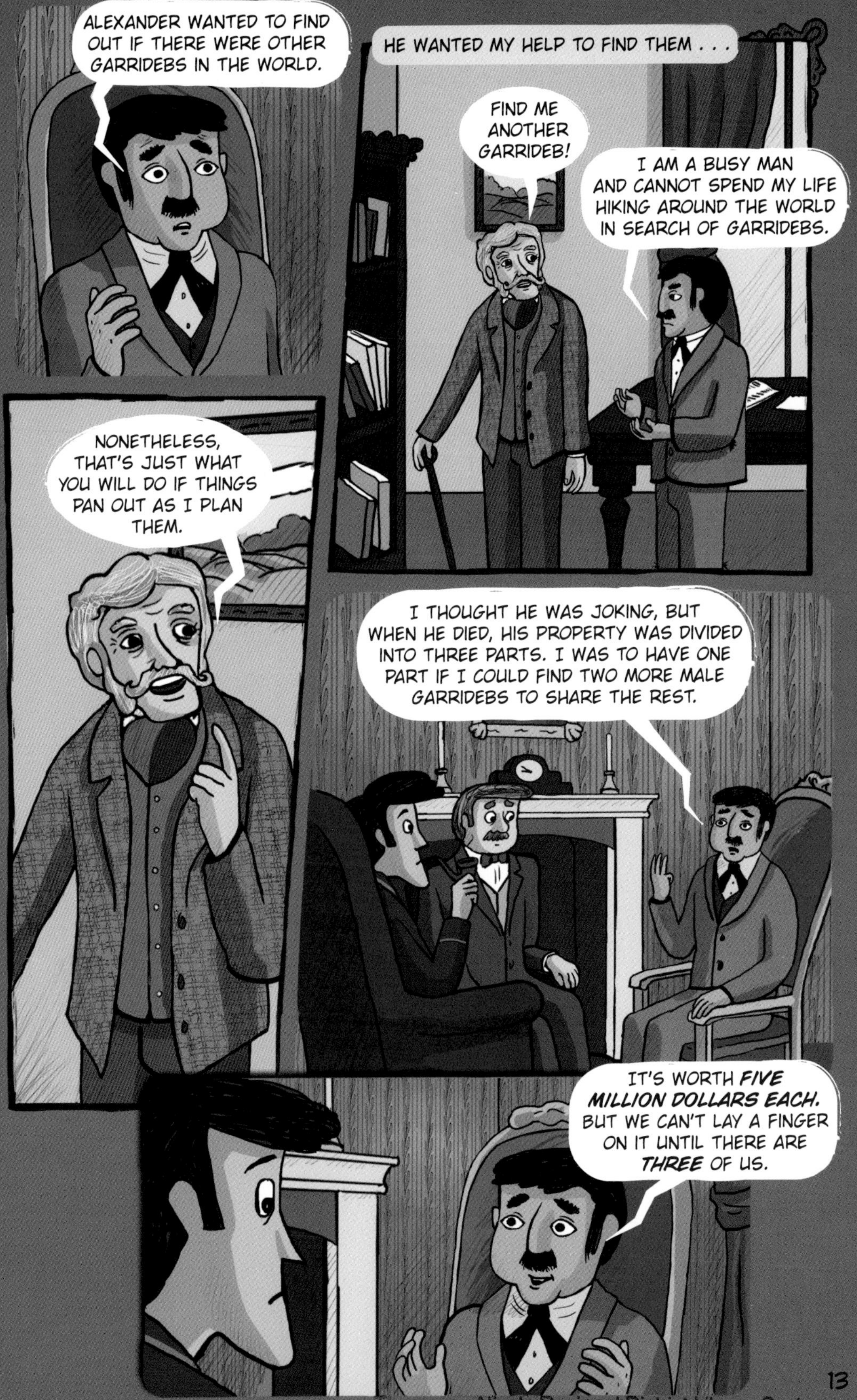
ALEXANDER WANTED TO FIND OUT IF THERE WERE OTHER GARRIDEBS IN THE WORLD.
HE WANTED MY HELP TO FIND THEM . . .
FIND ME ANOTHER GARRIDEB!
I AM A BUSY MAN AND CANNOT SPEND MY LIFE HIKING AROUND THE WORLD IN SEARCH OF GARRIDEBS.
NONETHELESS, THAT'S JUST WHAT YOU WILL DO IF THINGS PAN OUT AS I PLAN THEM.
I THOUGHT HE WAS JOKING, BUT WHEN HE DIED, HIS PROPERTY WAS DIVIDED INTO THREE PARTS. I WAS TO HAVE ONE PART IF I COULD FIND TWO MORE MALE GARRIDEBS TO SHARE THE REST.
IT'S WORTH *FIVE MILLION DOLLARS EACH.* BUT WE CAN'T LAY A FINGER ON IT UNTIL THERE ARE *THREE* OF US.

Our visitor explained that he had left his job and started looking for Garridebs. There was not another one in the United States. He went through the country with a fine-tooth comb, and never a Garrideb could he find. Then, he tried England. Sure enough, there was a name in the London telephone directory. He went after Nathan Garrideb two days ago and explained the whole matter to him. But like John Garrideb, Nathan is the only man left in his family. It states in the will that there must be three adult men. The two Garridebs had advertised in the papers but had no reply yet. John Garrideb told us that if we could help them find a third Garrideb, he and Nathan would pay our charges.

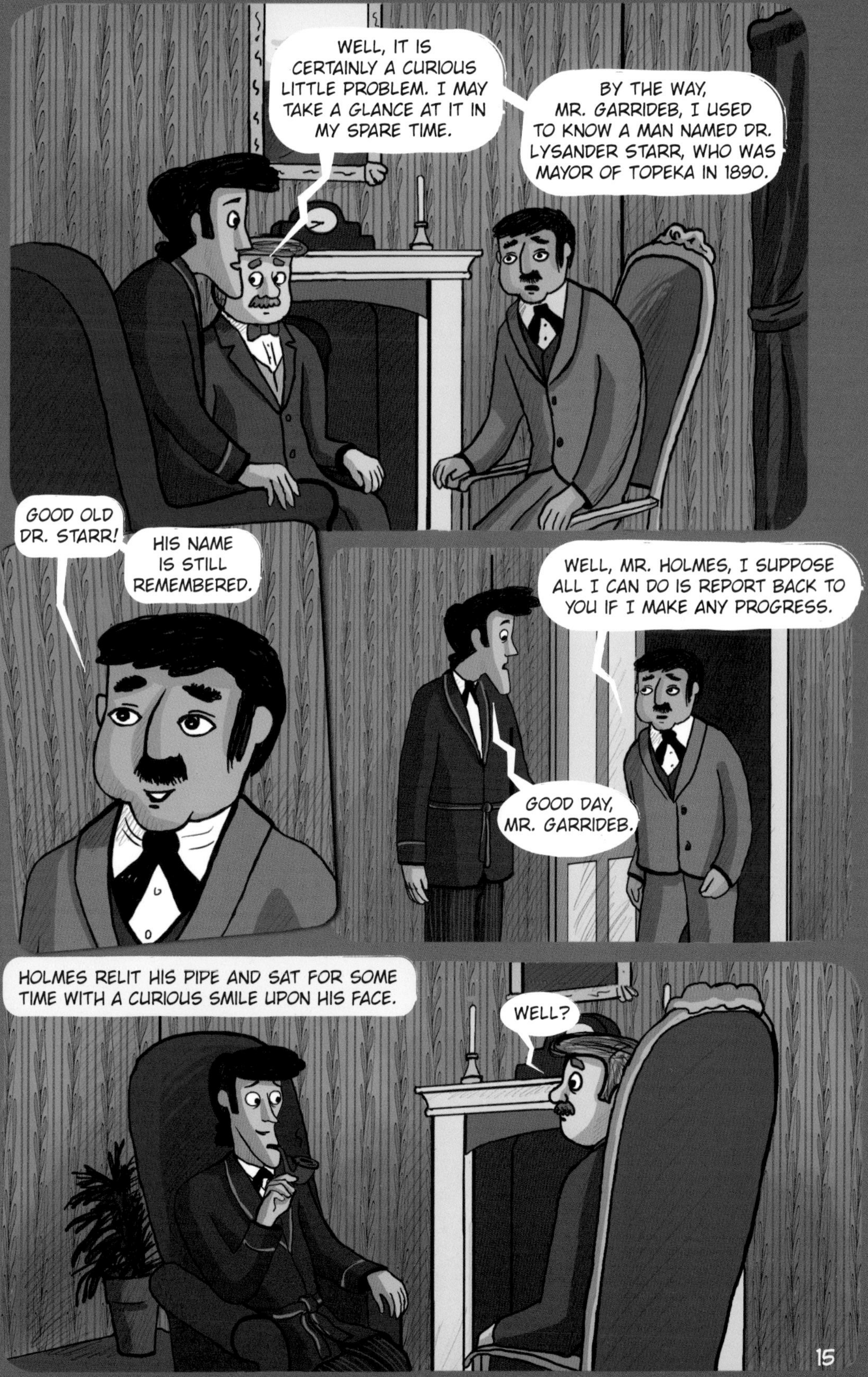

WELL, IT IS CERTAINLY A CURIOUS LITTLE PROBLEM. I MAY TAKE A GLANCE AT IT IN MY SPARE TIME.
BY THE WAY, MR. GARRIDEB, I USED TO KNOW A MAN NAMED DR. LYSANDER STARR, WHO WAS MAYOR OF TOPEKA IN 1890.
GOOD OLD DR. STARR!
HIS NAME IS STILL REMEMBERED.
WELL, MR. HOLMES, I SUPPOSE ALL I CAN DO IS REPORT BACK TO YOU IF I MAKE ANY PROGRESS.
GOOD DAY, MR. GARRIDEB.
HOLMES RELIT HIS PIPE AND SAT FOR SOME TIME WITH A CURIOUS SMILE UPON HIS FACE.
WELL?

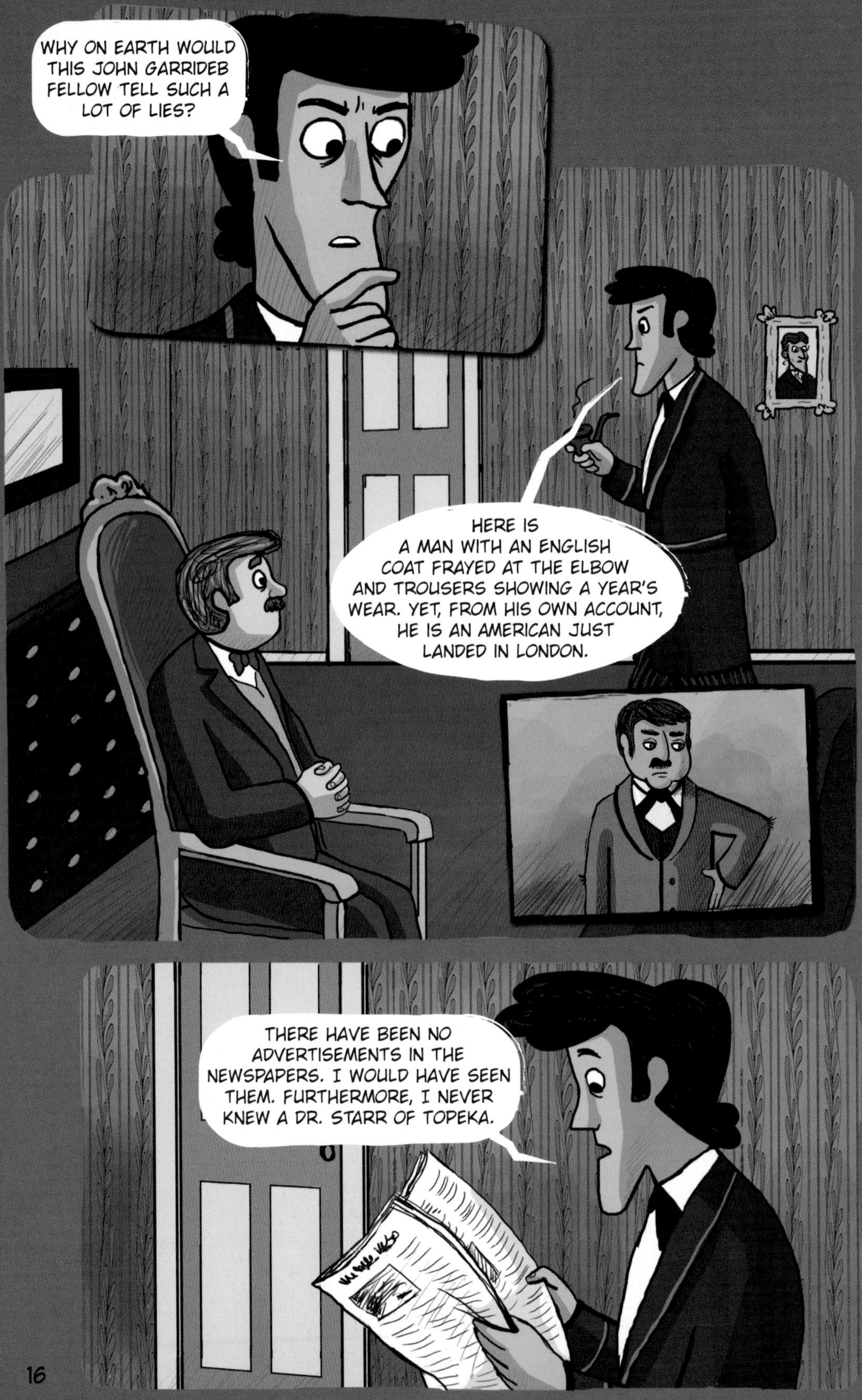
WHY ON EARTH WOULD THIS JOHN GARRIDEB FELLOW TELL SUCH A LOT OF LIES?
HERE IS A MAN WITH AN ENGLISH COAT FRAYED AT THE ELBOW AND TROUSERS SHOWING A YEAR'S WEAR. YET, FROM HIS OWN ACCOUNT, HE IS AN AMERICAN JUST LANDED IN LONDON.
THERE HAVE BEEN NO ADVERTISEMENTS IN THE NEWSPAPERS. I WOULD HAVE SEEN THEM. FURTHERMORE, I NEVER KNEW A DR. STARR OF TOPEKA.

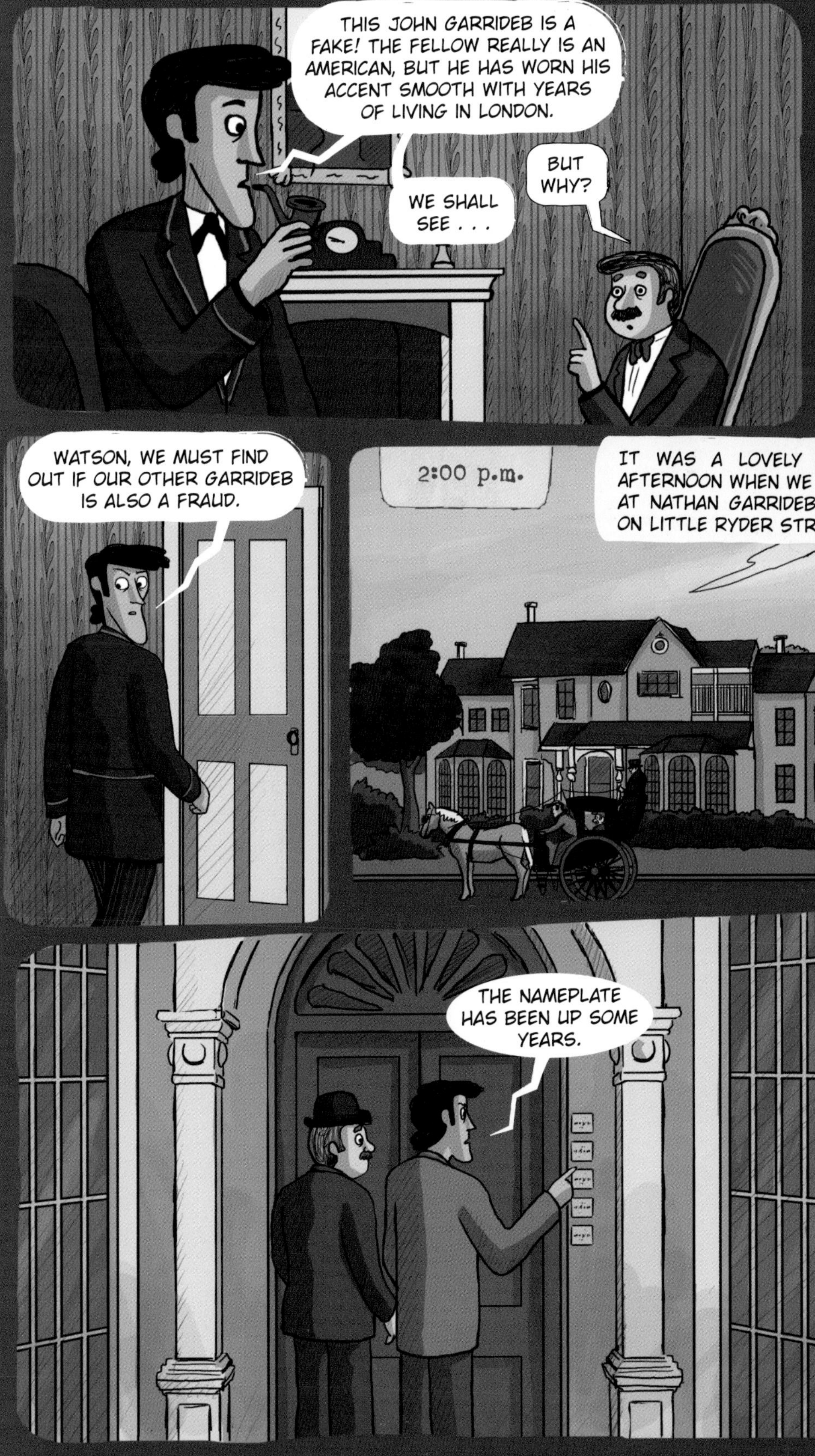
THIS JOHN GARRIDEB IS A FAKE! THE FELLOW REALLY IS AN AMERICAN, BUT HE HAS WORN HIS ACCENT SMOOTH WITH YEARS OF LIVING IN LONDON.
BUT WHY?
WE SHALL SEE . . .
WATSON, WE MUST FIND OUT IF OUR OTHER GARRIDEB IS ALSO A FRAUD.
2:00 p.m.
IT WAS A LOVELY SUMMER AFTERNOON WHEN WE ARRIVED AT NATHAN GARRIDEB'S HOME ON LITTLE RYDER STREET.
THE NAMEPLATE HAS BEEN UP SOME YEARS.

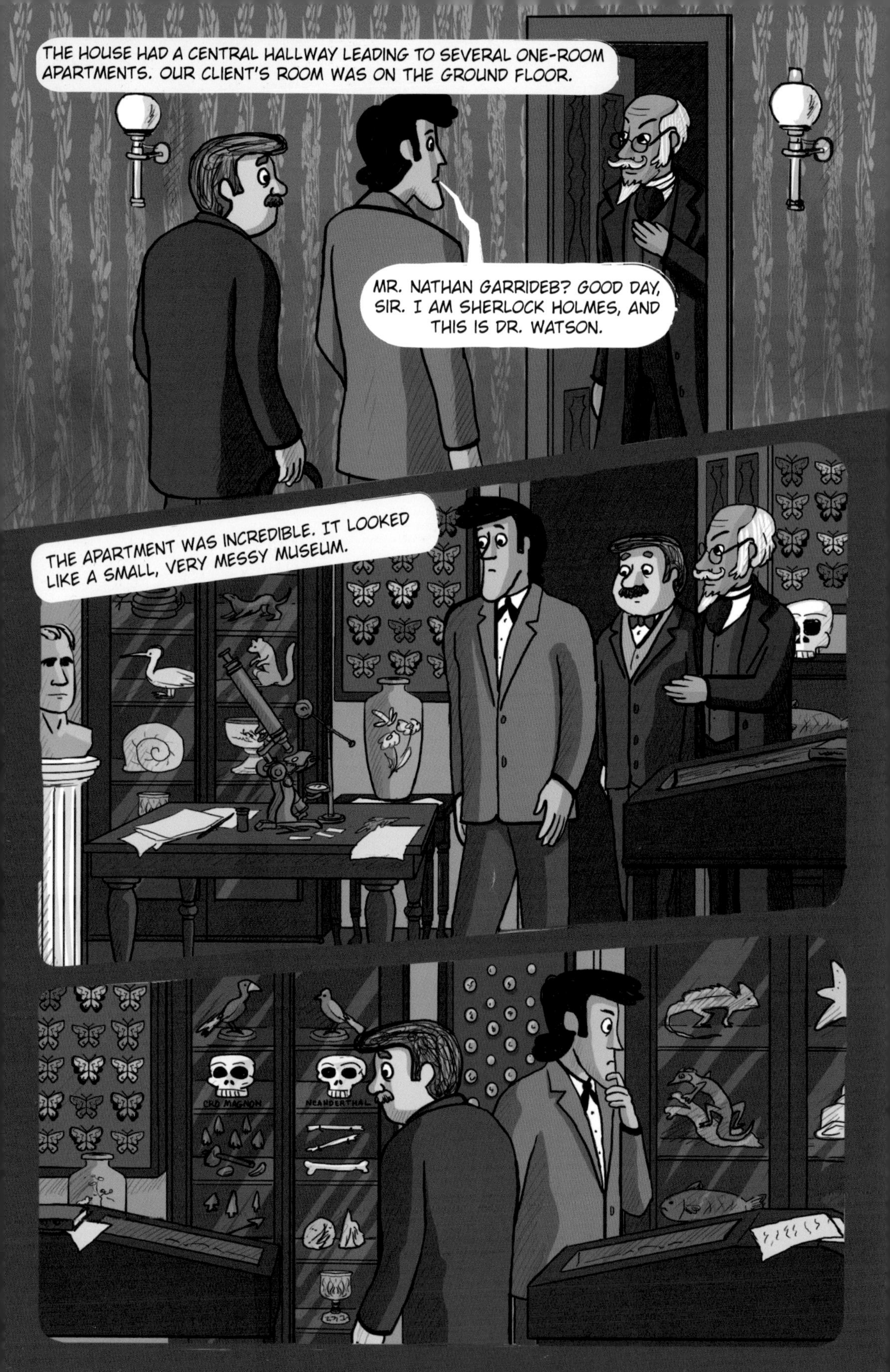
THE HOUSE HAD A CENTRAL HALLWAY LEADING TO SEVERAL ONE-ROOM APARTMENTS. OUR CLIENT'S ROOM WAS ON THE GROUND FLOOR.
MR. NATHAN GARRIDEB? GOOD DAY, SIR. I AM SHERLOCK HOLMES, AND THIS IS DR. WATSON.
THE APARTMENT WAS INCREDIBLE. IT LOOKED LIKE A SMALL, VERY MESSY MUSEUM.
CRO MAGNON
NEANDERTHAL

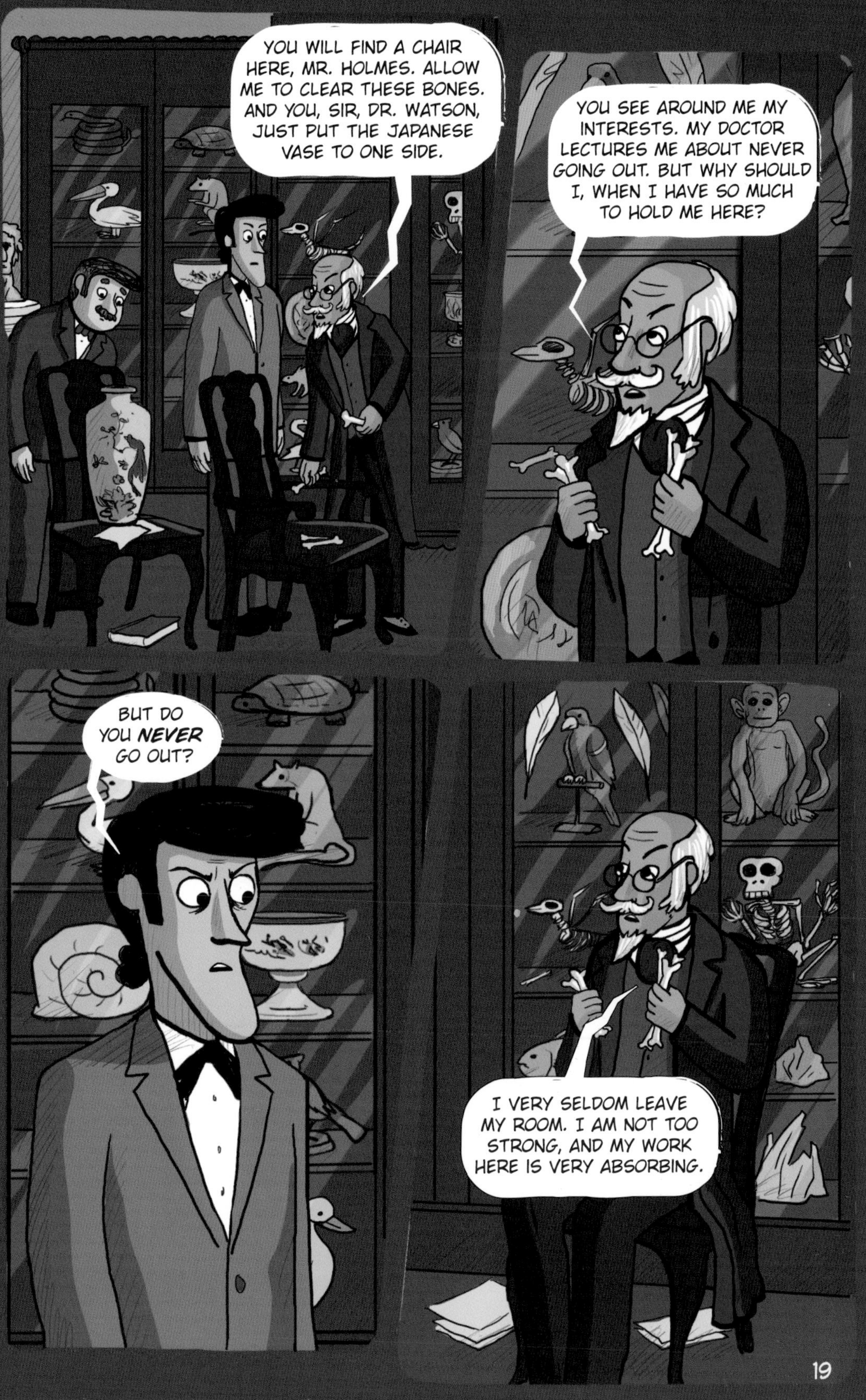
YOU WILL FIND A CHAIR HERE, MR. HOLMES. ALLOW ME TO CLEAR THESE BONES. AND YOU, SIR, DR. WATSON, JUST PUT THE JAPANESE VASE TO ONE SIDE.
YOU SEE AROUND ME MY INTERESTS. MY DOCTOR LECTURES ME ABOUT NEVER GOING OUT. BUT WHY SHOULD I, WHEN I HAVE SO MUCH TO HOLD ME HERE?
BUT DO YOU ***NEVER*** GO OUT?
I VERY SELDOM LEAVE MY ROOM. I AM NOT TOO STRONG, AND MY WORK HERE IS VERY ABSORBING.

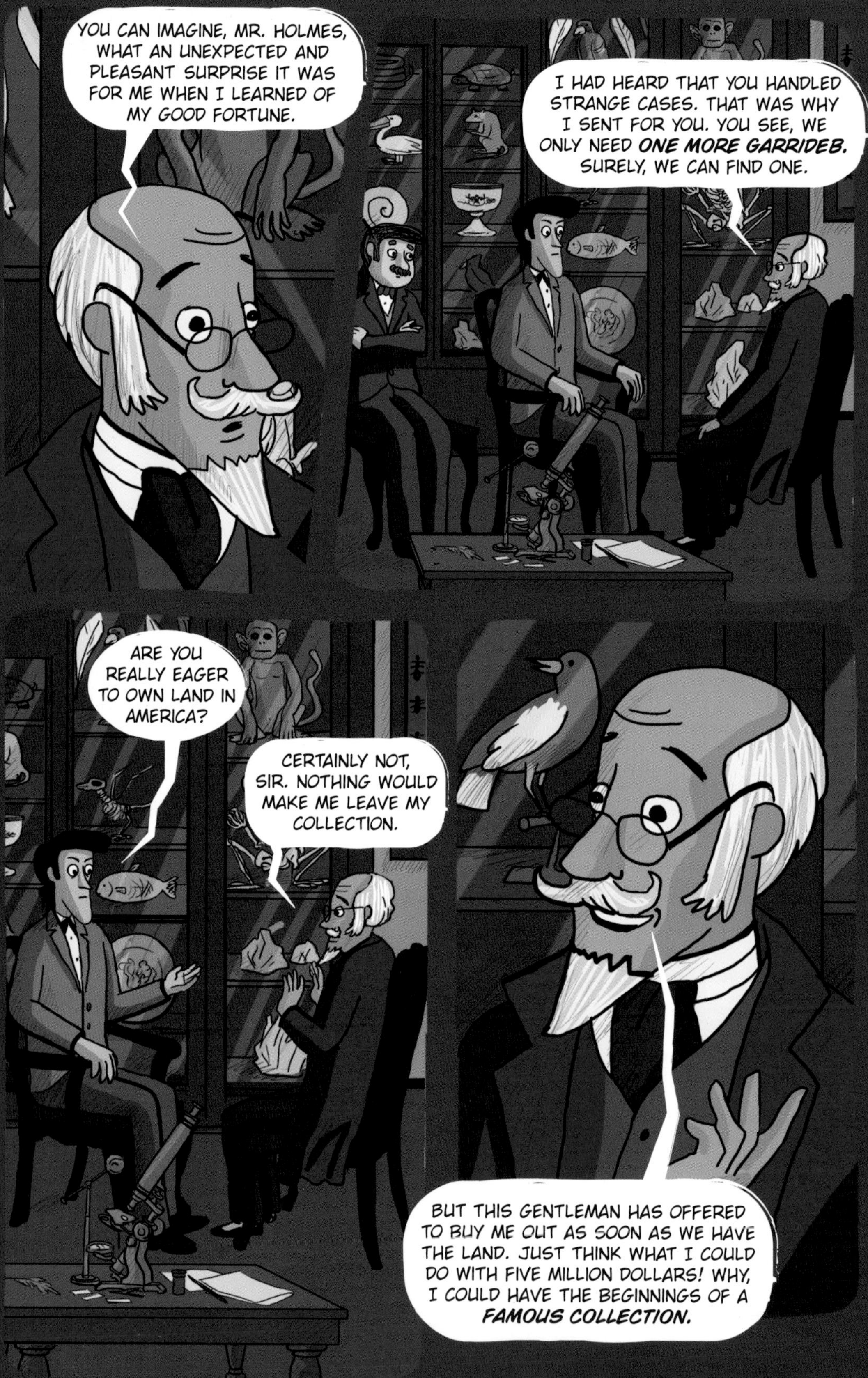
YOU CAN IMAGINE, MR. HOLMES, WHAT AN UNEXPECTED AND PLEASANT SURPRISE IT WAS FOR ME WHEN I LEARNED OF MY GOOD FORTUNE.
I HAD HEARD THAT YOU HANDLED STRANGE CASES. THAT WAS WHY I SENT FOR YOU. YOU SEE, WE ONLY NEED ONE MORE GARRIDEB. SURELY, WE CAN FIND ONE.
ARE YOU REALLY EAGER TO OWN LAND IN AMERICA?
CERTAINLY NOT, SIR. NOTHING WOULD MAKE ME LEAVE MY COLLECTION.
BUT THIS GENTLEMAN HAS OFFERED TO BUY ME OUT AS SOON AS WE HAVE THE LAND. JUST THINK WHAT I COULD DO WITH FIVE MILLION DOLLARS! WHY, I COULD HAVE THE BEGINNINGS OF A FAMOUS COLLECTION.

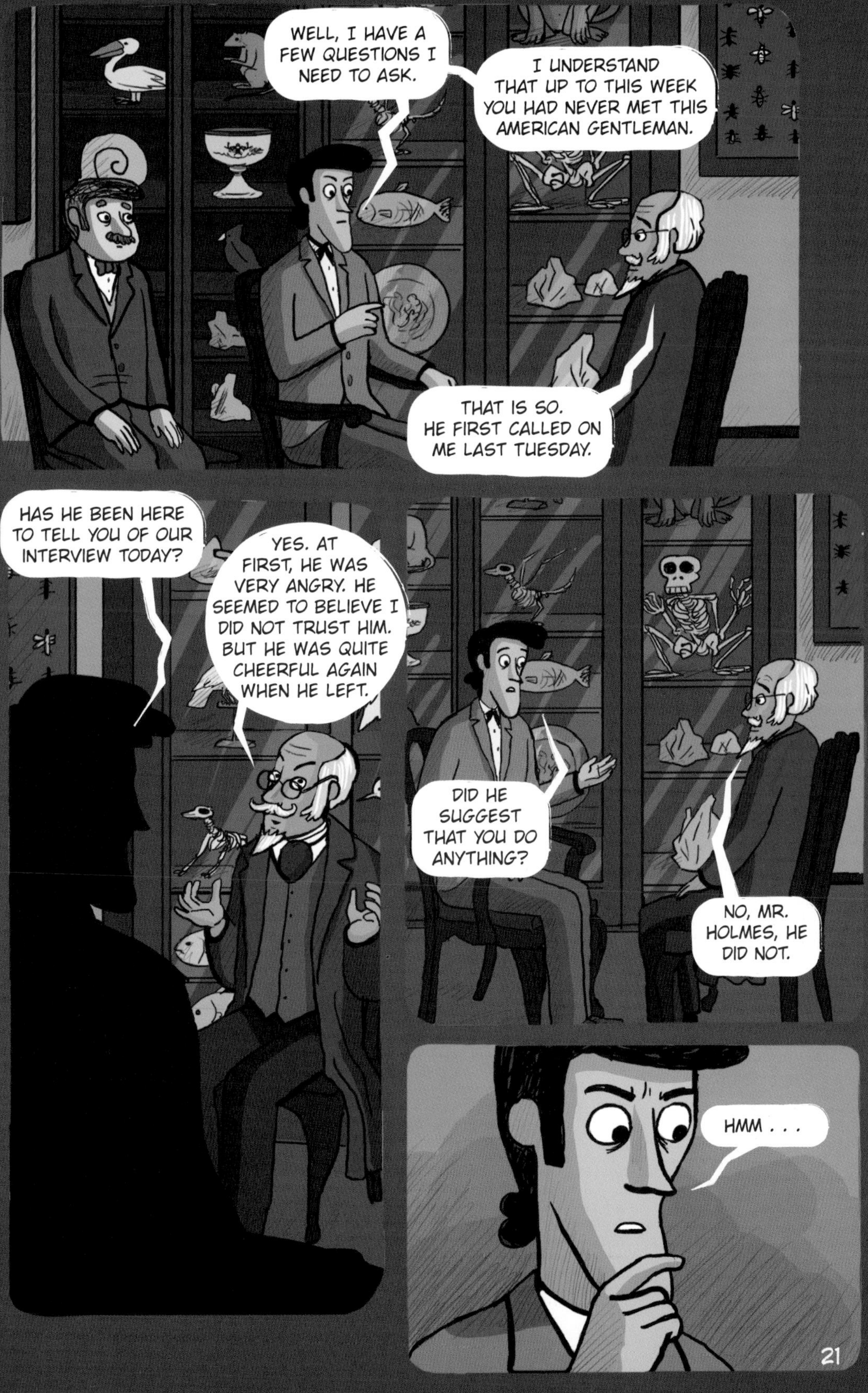
WELL, I HAVE A FEW QUESTIONS I NEED TO ASK.
I UNDERSTAND THAT UP TO THIS WEEK YOU HAD NEVER MET THIS AMERICAN GENTLEMAN.
THAT IS SO. HE FIRST CALLED ON ME LAST TUESDAY.
HAS HE BEEN HERE TO TELL YOU OF OUR INTERVIEW TODAY?
YES. AT FIRST, HE WAS VERY ANGRY. HE SEEMED TO BELIEVE I DID NOT TRUST HIM. BUT HE WAS QUITE CHEERFUL AGAIN WHEN HE LEFT.
DID HE SUGGEST THAT YOU DO ANYTHING?
NO, MR. HOLMES, HE DID NOT.
HMM . . .

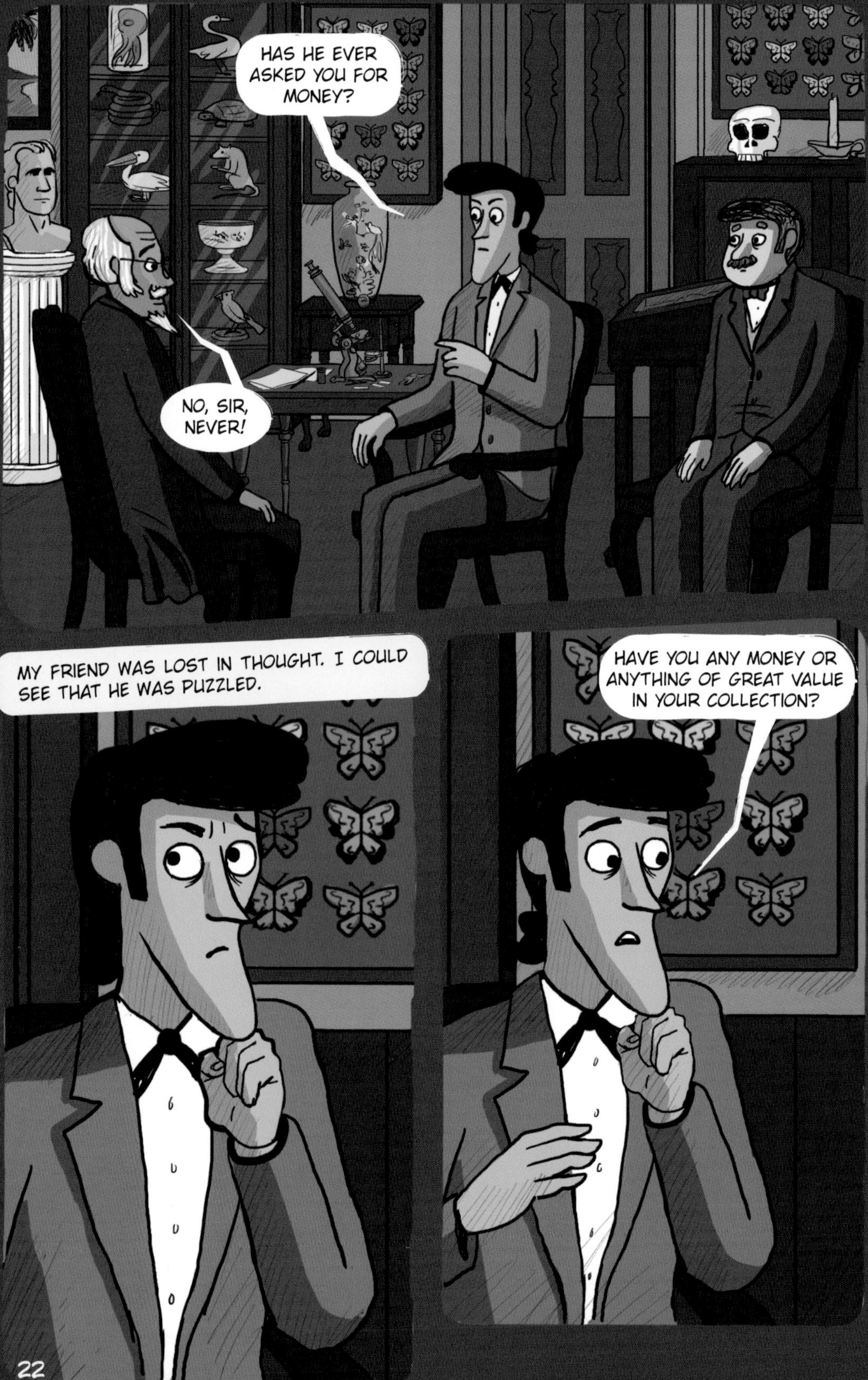
HAS HE EVER ASKED YOU FOR MONEY?
NO, SIR, NEVER!
MY FRIEND WAS LOST IN THOUGHT. I COULD SEE THAT HE WAS PUZZLED.
HAVE YOU ANY MONEY OR ANYTHING OF GREAT VALUE IN YOUR COLLECTION?

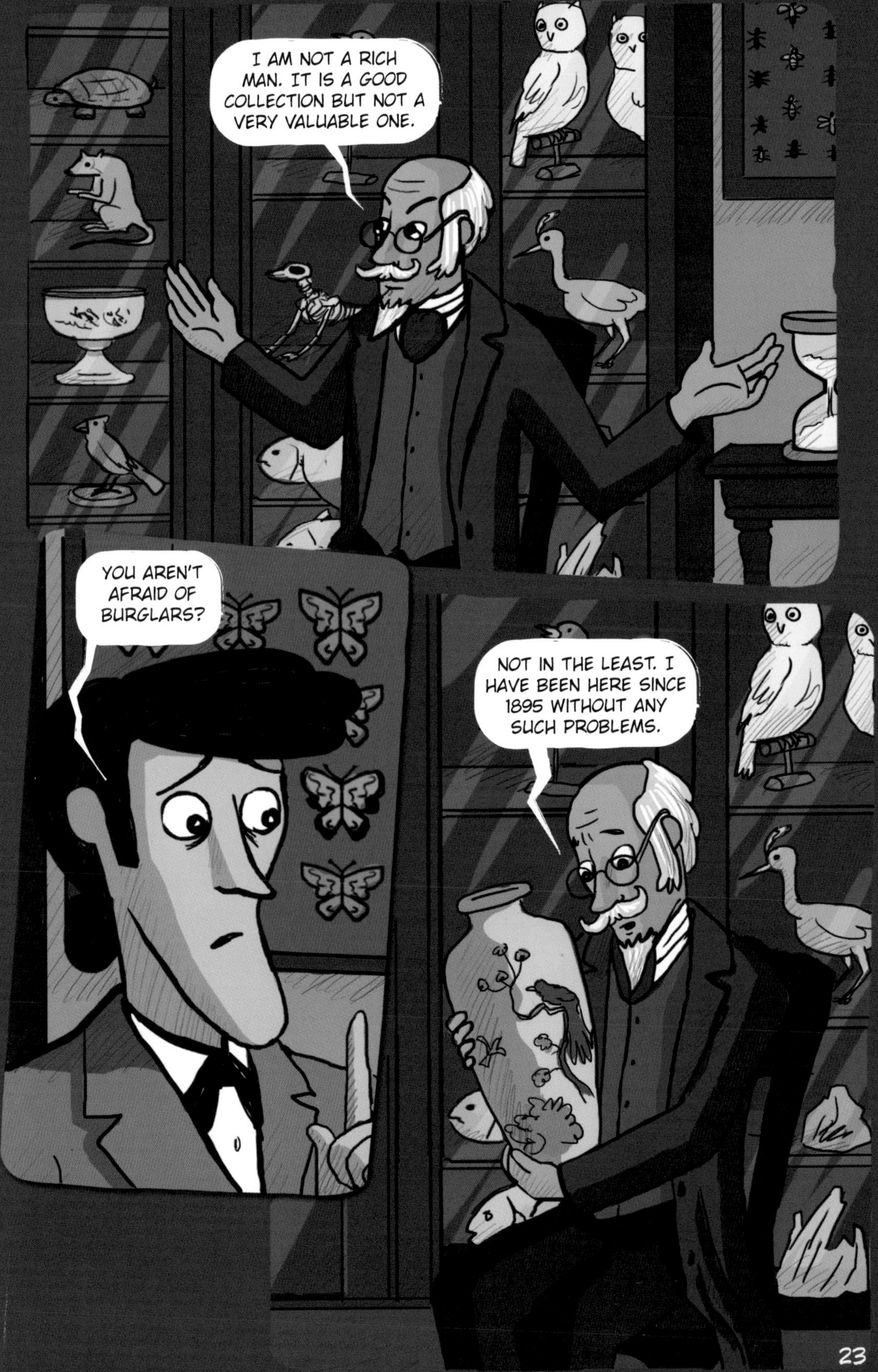
I AM NOT A RICH MAN. IT IS A GOOD COLLECTION BUT NOT A VERY VALUABLE ONE.
YOU AREN'T AFRAID OF BURGLARS?
NOT IN THE LEAST. I HAVE BEEN HERE SINCE 1895 WITHOUT ANY SUCH PROBLEMS.

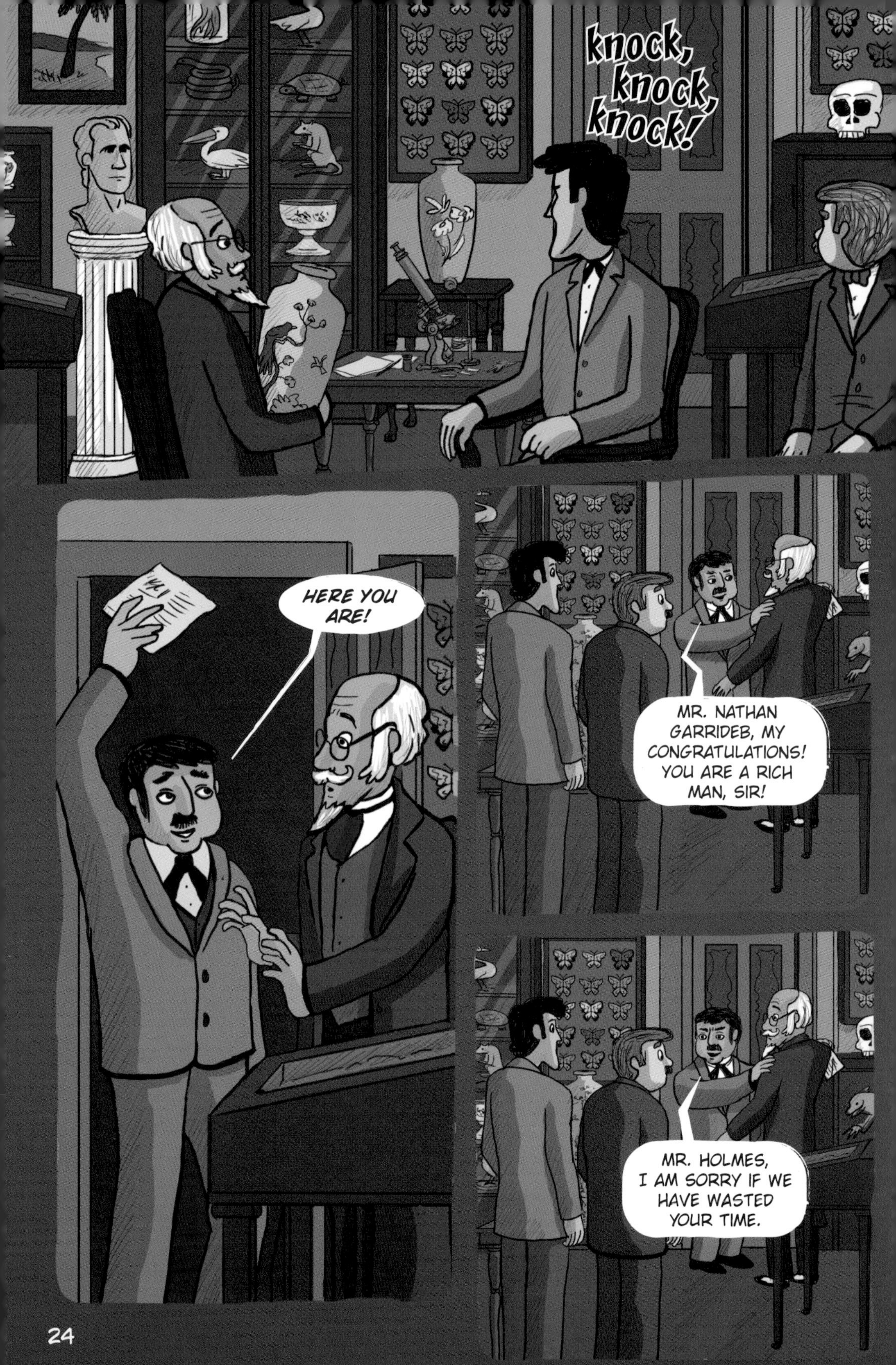
knock, knock, knock!
HERE YOU ARE!
MR. NATHAN GARRIDEB, MY CONGRATULATIONS! YOU ARE A RICH MAN, SIR!
MR. HOLMES, I AM SORRY IF WE HAVE WASTED YOUR TIME.

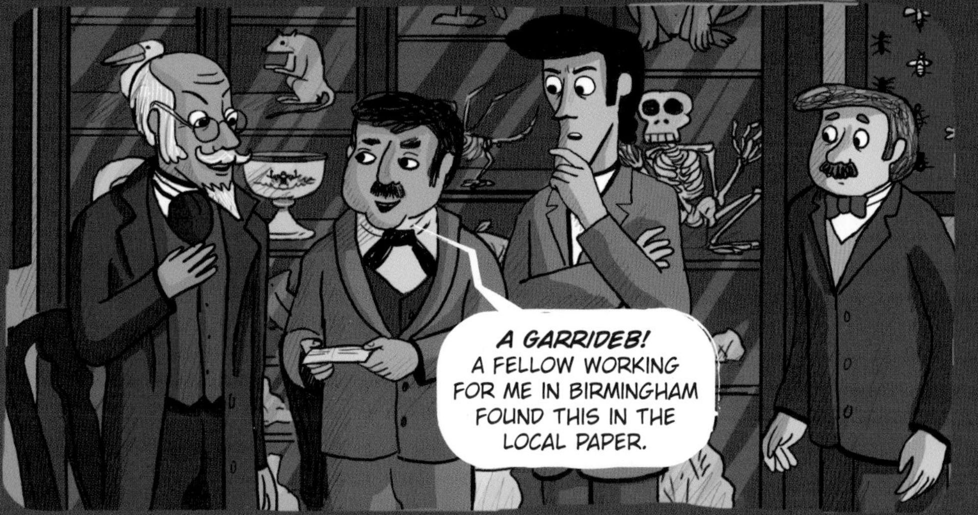
A GARRIDEB! A FELLOW WORKING FOR ME IN BIRMINGHAM FOUND THIS IN THE LOCAL PAPER.

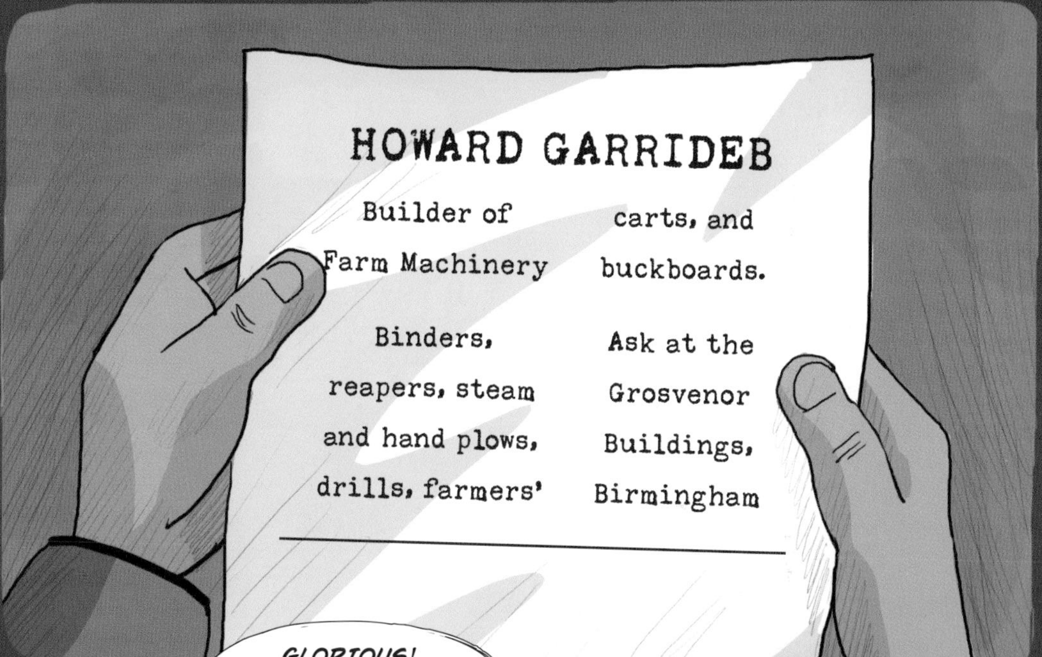
HOWARD GARRIDEB
Builder of Farm Machinery
Binders, reapers, steam and hand plows, drills, farmers' carts, and buckboards.
Ask at the Grosvenor Buildings, Birmingham

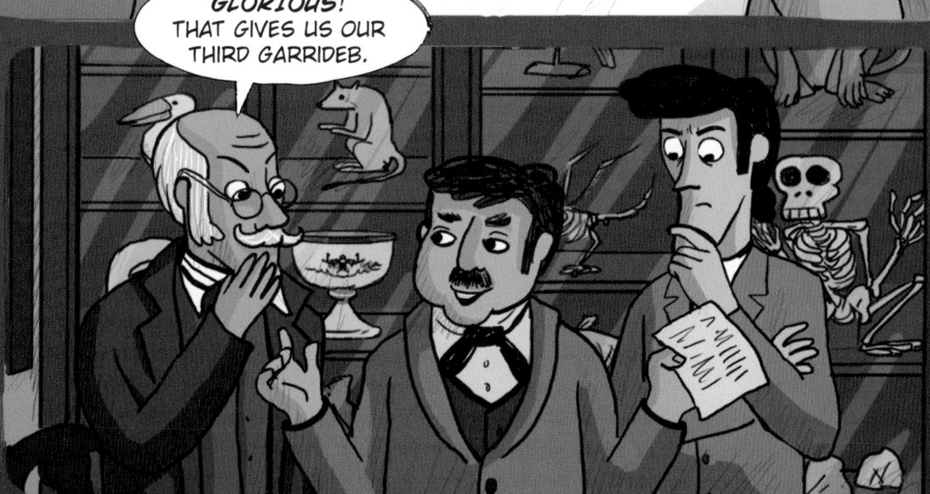
GLORIOUS! THAT GIVES US OUR THIRD GARRIDEB.

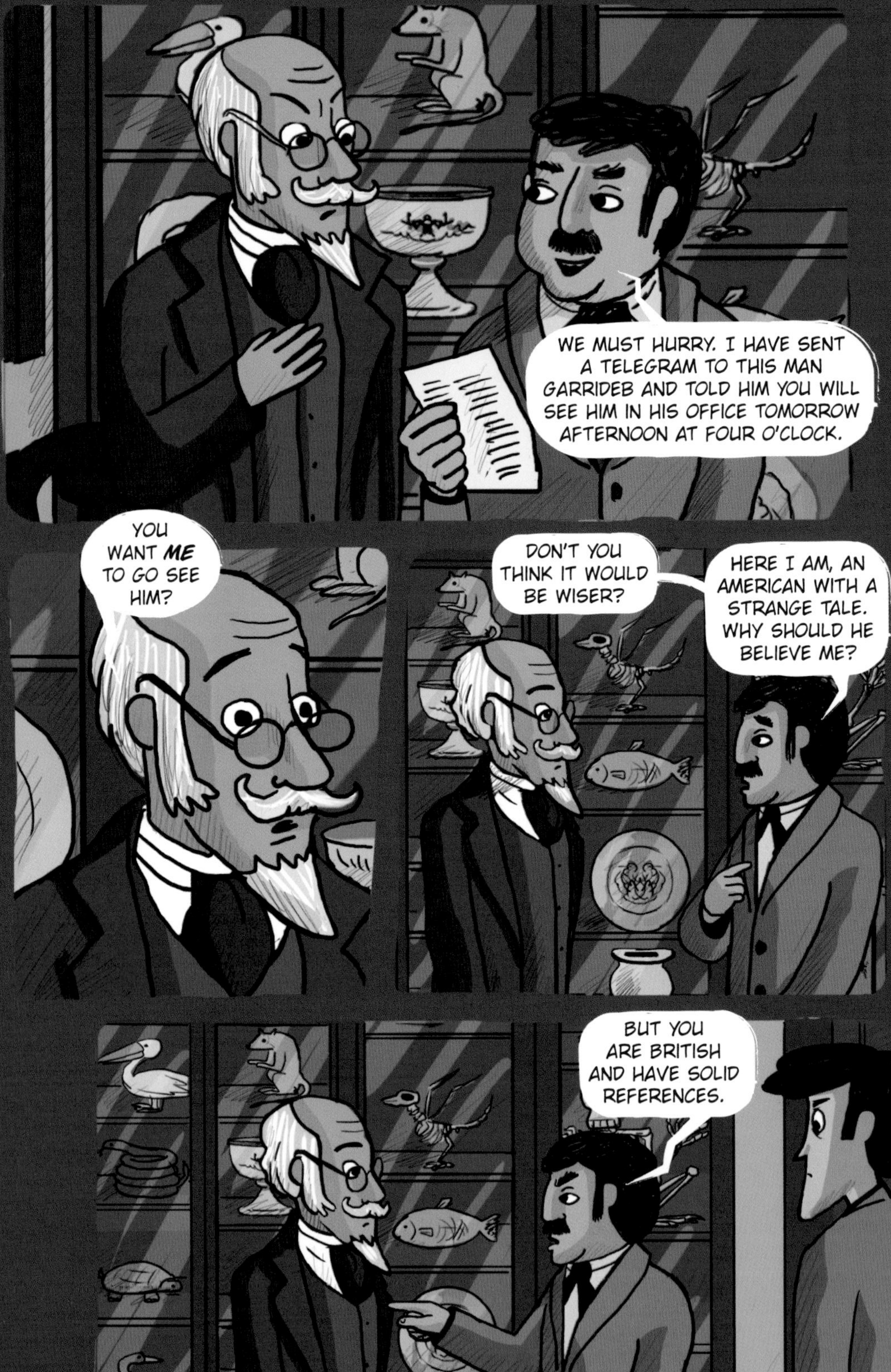

WE MUST HURRY. I HAVE SENT A TELEGRAM TO THIS MAN GARRIDEB AND TOLD HIM YOU WILL SEE HIM IN HIS OFFICE TOMORROW AFTERNOON AT FOUR O'CLOCK.
YOU WANT ***ME*** TO GO SEE HIM?
DON'T YOU THINK IT WOULD BE WISER?
HERE I AM, AN AMERICAN WITH A STRANGE TALE. WHY SHOULD HE BELIEVE ME?
BUT YOU ARE BRITISH AND HAVE SOLID REFERENCES.

I WOULD GO WITH YOU, BUT I'M VERY BUSY TOMORROW.
I HAVE NOT MADE SUCH A JOURNEY FOR YEARS.
UPON MY WORD! CONSIDERING I'VE COME ALL THE WAY FROM AMERICA, IT IS SURELY LITTLE ENOUGH IF YOU GO A HUNDRED MILES.
QUITE SO.

WELL, IF YOU INSIST, I SHALL GO. IT IS CERTAINLY HARD FOR ME TO REFUSE YOU ANYTHING, CONSIDERING THE HOPE YOU HAVE BROUGHT INTO MY LIFE.

THEN THAT IS AGREED.

LET ME HAVE A REPORT AS SOON AS YOU CAN.

I'LL SEE TO THAT.

WELL, I'LL HAVE TO GET ON.

WE WILL BE IN TOUCH TOMORROW, THEN.

I WISH I COULD LOOK OVER YOUR COLLECTION, MR. GARRIDEB. MAY I LOOK IN TOMORROW AFTERNOON?

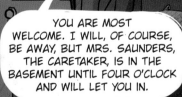
YOU ARE MOST WELCOME. I WILL, OF COURSE, BE AWAY, BUT MRS. SAUNDERS, THE CARETAKER, IS IN THE BASEMENT UNTIL FOUR O'CLOCK AND WILL LET YOU IN.

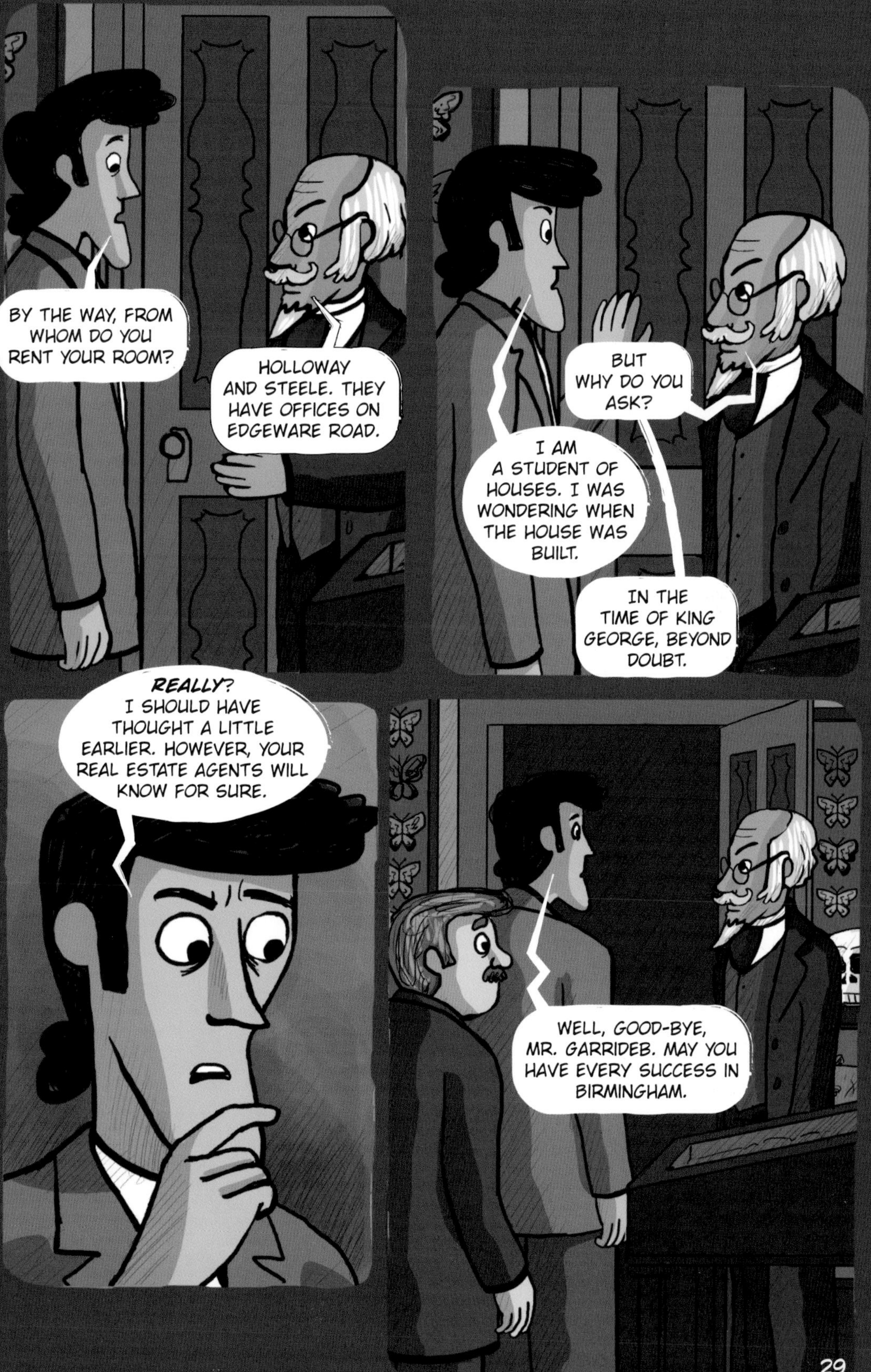
BY THE WAY, FROM WHOM DO YOU RENT YOUR ROOM?
HOLLOWAY AND STEELE. THEY HAVE OFFICES ON EDGEWARE ROAD.
BUT WHY DO YOU ASK?
I AM A STUDENT OF HOUSES. I WAS WONDERING WHEN THE HOUSE WAS BUILT.
IN THE TIME OF KING GEORGE, BEYOND DOUBT.
REALLY? I SHOULD HAVE THOUGHT A LITTLE EARLIER. HOWEVER, YOUR REAL ESTATE AGENTS WILL KNOW FOR SURE.
WELL, GOOD-BYE, MR. GARRIDEB. MAY YOU HAVE EVERY SUCCESS IN BIRMINGHAM.

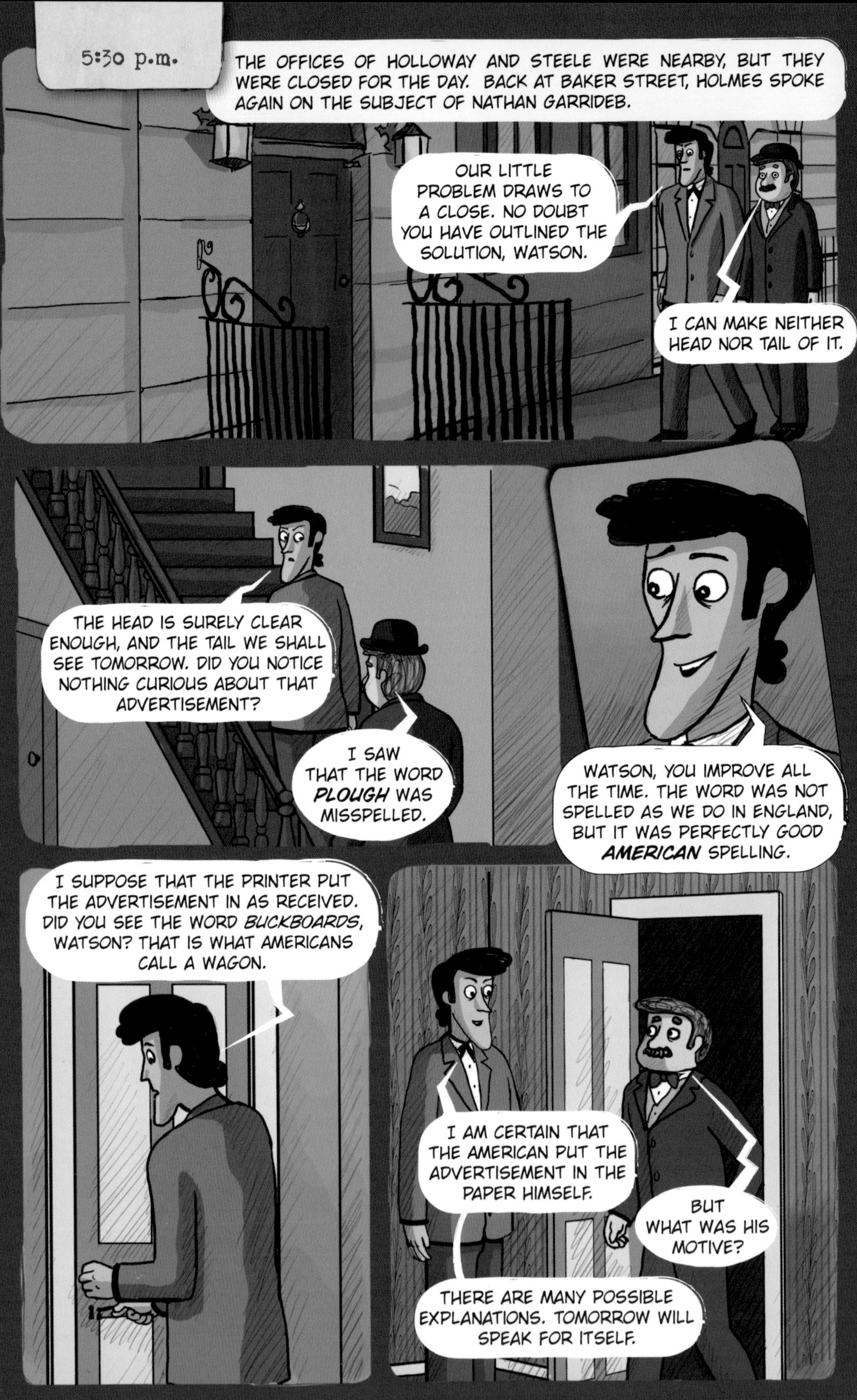
5:30 p.m.
THE OFFICES OF HOLLOWAY AND STEELE WERE NEARBY, BUT THEY WERE CLOSED FOR THE DAY. BACK AT BAKER STREET, HOLMES SPOKE AGAIN ON THE SUBJECT OF NATHAN GARRIDEB.
OUR LITTLE PROBLEM DRAWS TO A CLOSE. NO DOUBT YOU HAVE OUTLINED THE SOLUTION, WATSON.
I CAN MAKE NEITHER HEAD NOR TAIL OF IT.
THE HEAD IS SURELY CLEAR ENOUGH, AND THE TAIL WE SHALL SEE TOMORROW. DID YOU NOTICE NOTHING CURIOUS ABOUT THAT ADVERTISEMENT?
I SAW THAT THE WORD ***PLOUGH*** WAS MISSPELLED.
WATSON, YOU IMPROVE ALL THE TIME. THE WORD WAS NOT SPELLED AS WE DO IN ENGLAND, BUT IT WAS PERFECTLY GOOD ***AMERICAN*** SPELLING.
I SUPPOSE THAT THE PRINTER PUT THE ADVERTISEMENT IN AS RECEIVED. DID YOU SEE THE WORD *BUCKBOARDS*, WATSON? THAT IS WHAT AMERICANS CALL A WAGON.
I AM CERTAIN THAT THE AMERICAN PUT THE ADVERTISEMENT IN THE PAPER HIMSELF.
BUT WHAT WAS HIS MOTIVE?
THERE ARE MANY POSSIBLE EXPLANATIONS. TOMORROW WILL SPEAK FOR ITSELF.

June 24, 1902

Holmes was up and out early the next day. When he returned at lunchtime, his face was very grave. He explained that the case was far more serious than he had expected. He had been to Scotland Yard and had found that our American friend was in their photographic records. Holmes read the following from his notes: "James Winter, alias Morecroft, alias Killer Evans. Aged forty-four. Native of Chicago. Came to London in 1893. Shot a man in an argument in January 1895. Man died and was identified as Roger Prescott, a famous maker of counterfeit money. Evans was sent to jail but recently escaped. Very dangerous man. Known to carry a gun and prepared to use it."

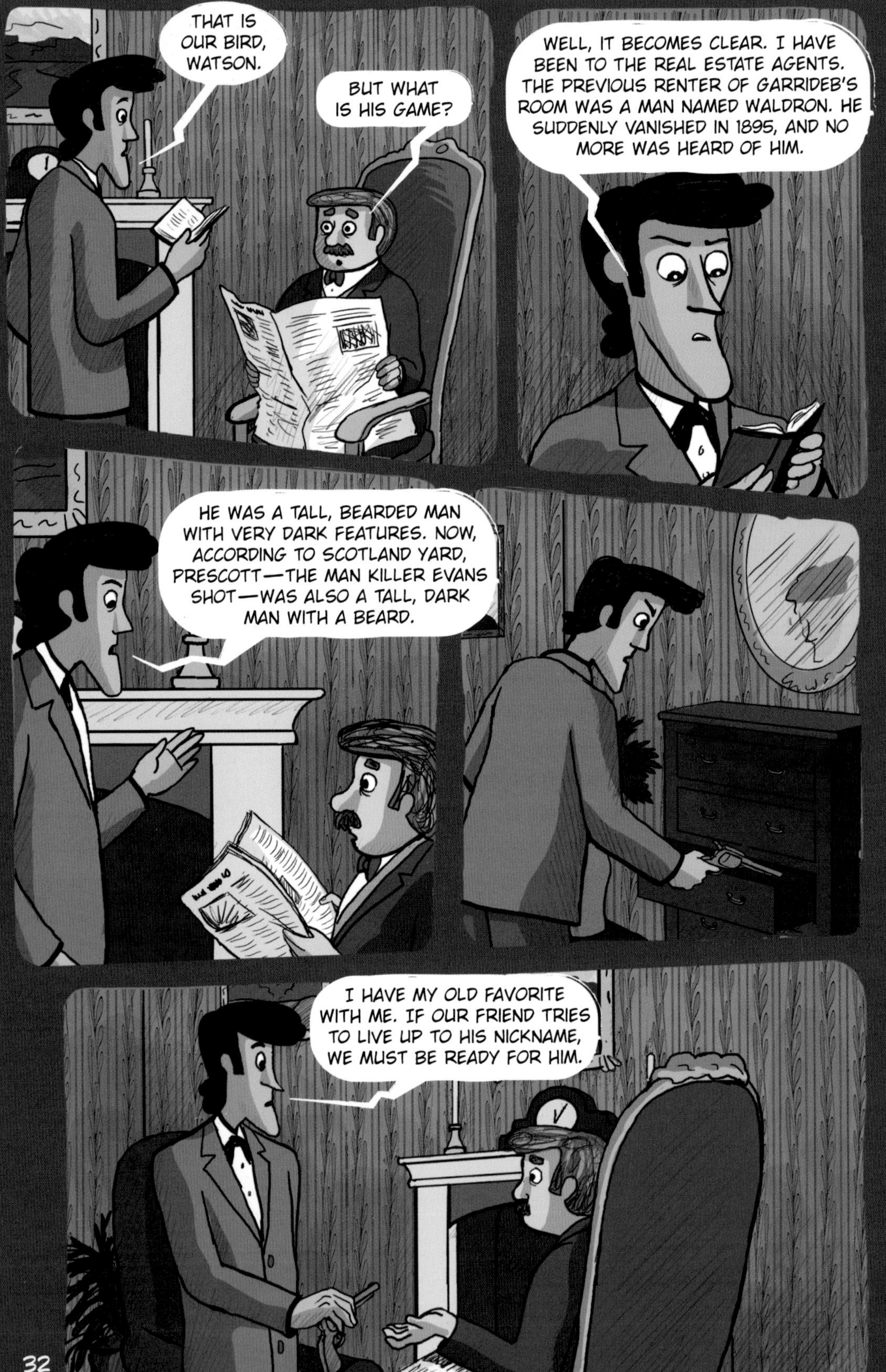
THAT IS OUR BIRD, WATSON.
BUT WHAT IS HIS GAME?
WELL, IT BECOMES CLEAR. I HAVE BEEN TO THE REAL ESTATE AGENTS. THE PREVIOUS RENTER OF GARRIDEB'S ROOM WAS A MAN NAMED WALDRON. HE SUDDENLY VANISHED IN 1895, AND NO MORE WAS HEARD OF HIM.
HE WAS A TALL, BEARDED MAN WITH VERY DARK FEATURES. NOW, ACCORDING TO SCOTLAND YARD, PRESCOTT—THE MAN KILLER EVANS SHOT—WAS ALSO A TALL, DARK MAN WITH A BEARD.
I HAVE MY OLD FAVORITE WITH ME. IF OUR FRIEND TRIES TO LIVE UP TO HIS NICKNAME, WE MUST BE READY FOR HIM.

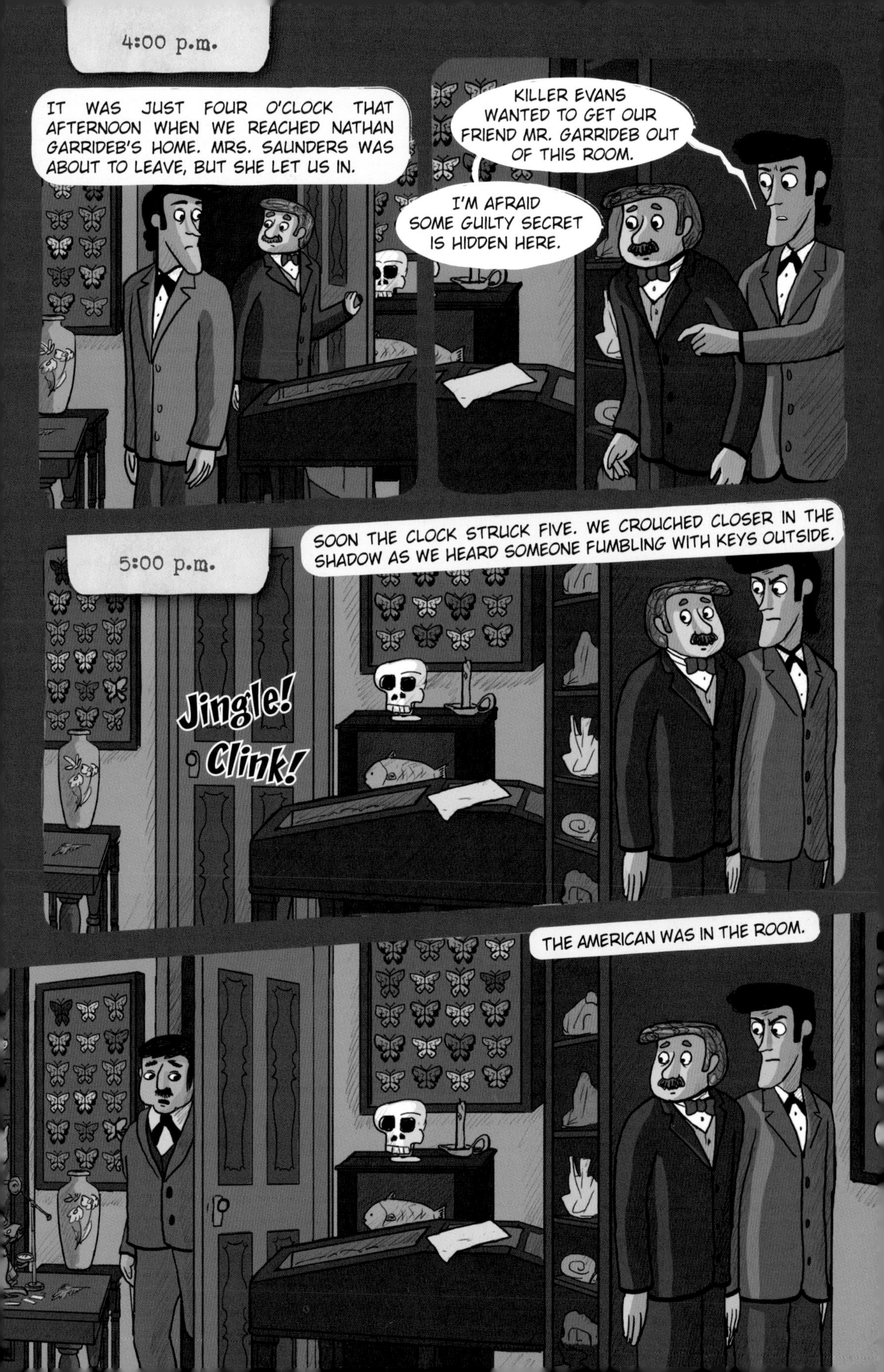
4:00 p.m.
IT WAS JUST FOUR O'CLOCK THAT AFTERNOON WHEN WE REACHED NATHAN GARRIDEB'S HOME. MRS. SAUNDERS WAS ABOUT TO LEAVE, BUT SHE LET US IN.
KILLER EVANS WANTED TO GET OUR FRIEND MR. GARRIDEB OUT OF THIS ROOM.
I'M AFRAID SOME GUILTY SECRET IS HIDDEN HERE.
5:00 p.m.
SOON THE CLOCK STRUCK FIVE. WE CROUCHED CLOSER IN THE SHADOW AS WE HEARD SOMEONE FUMBLING WITH KEYS OUTSIDE.
Jingle!
Clink!
THE AMERICAN WAS IN THE ROOM.

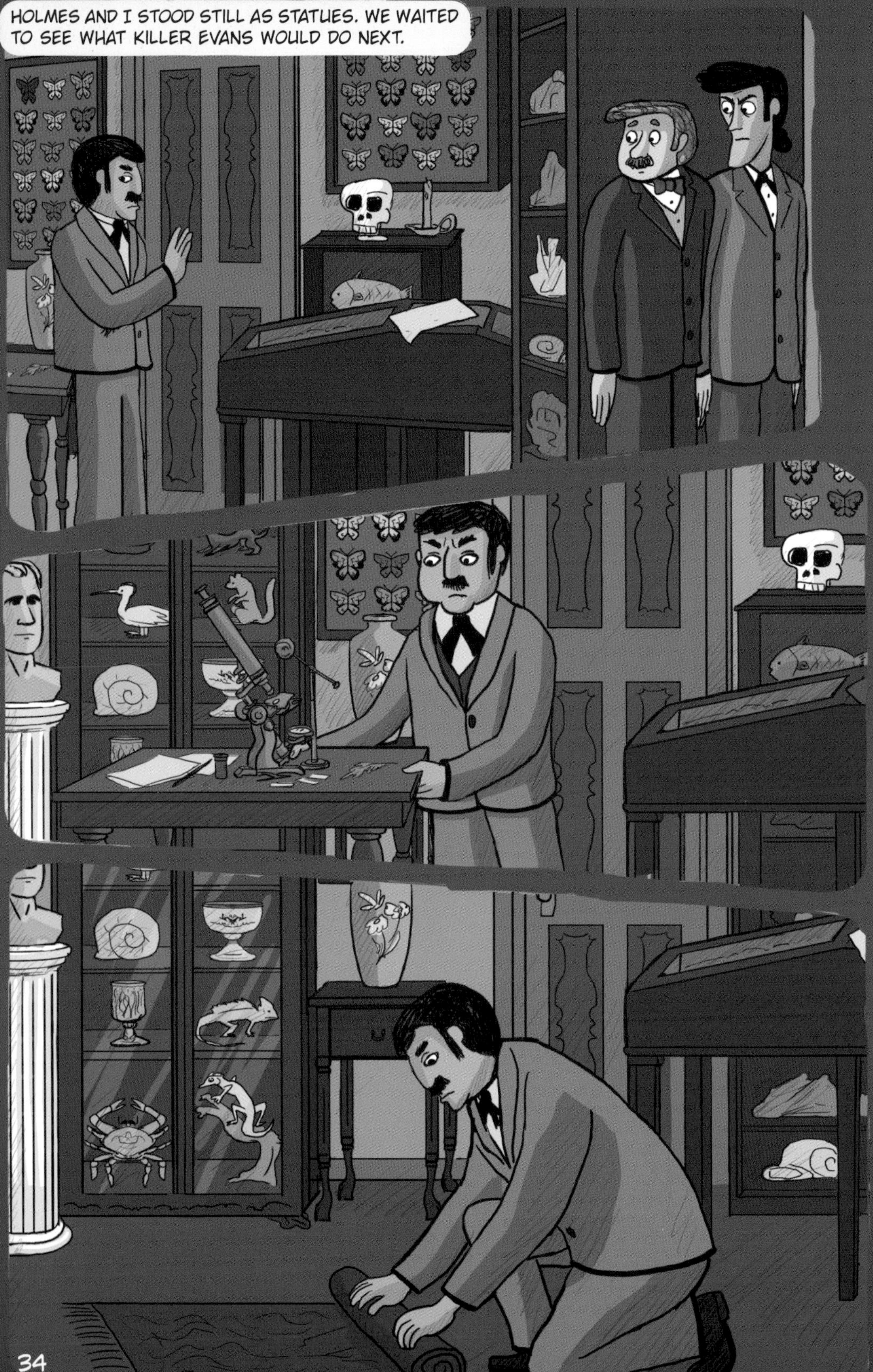
HOLMES AND I STOOD STILL AS STATUES. WE WAITED TO SEE WHAT KILLER EVANS WOULD DO NEXT.

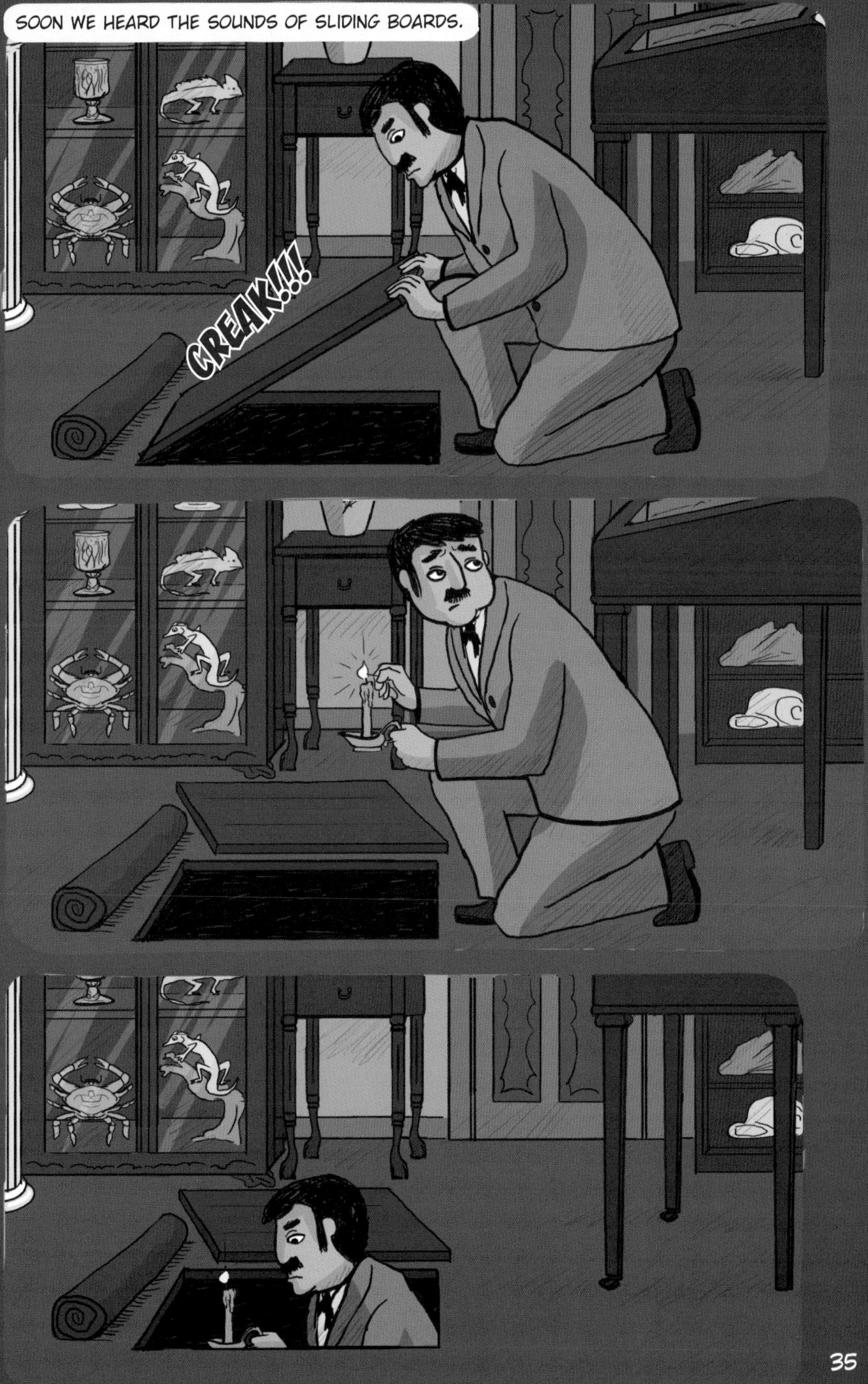
SOON WE HEARD THE SOUNDS OF SLIDING BOARDS.
CREAK!!!!

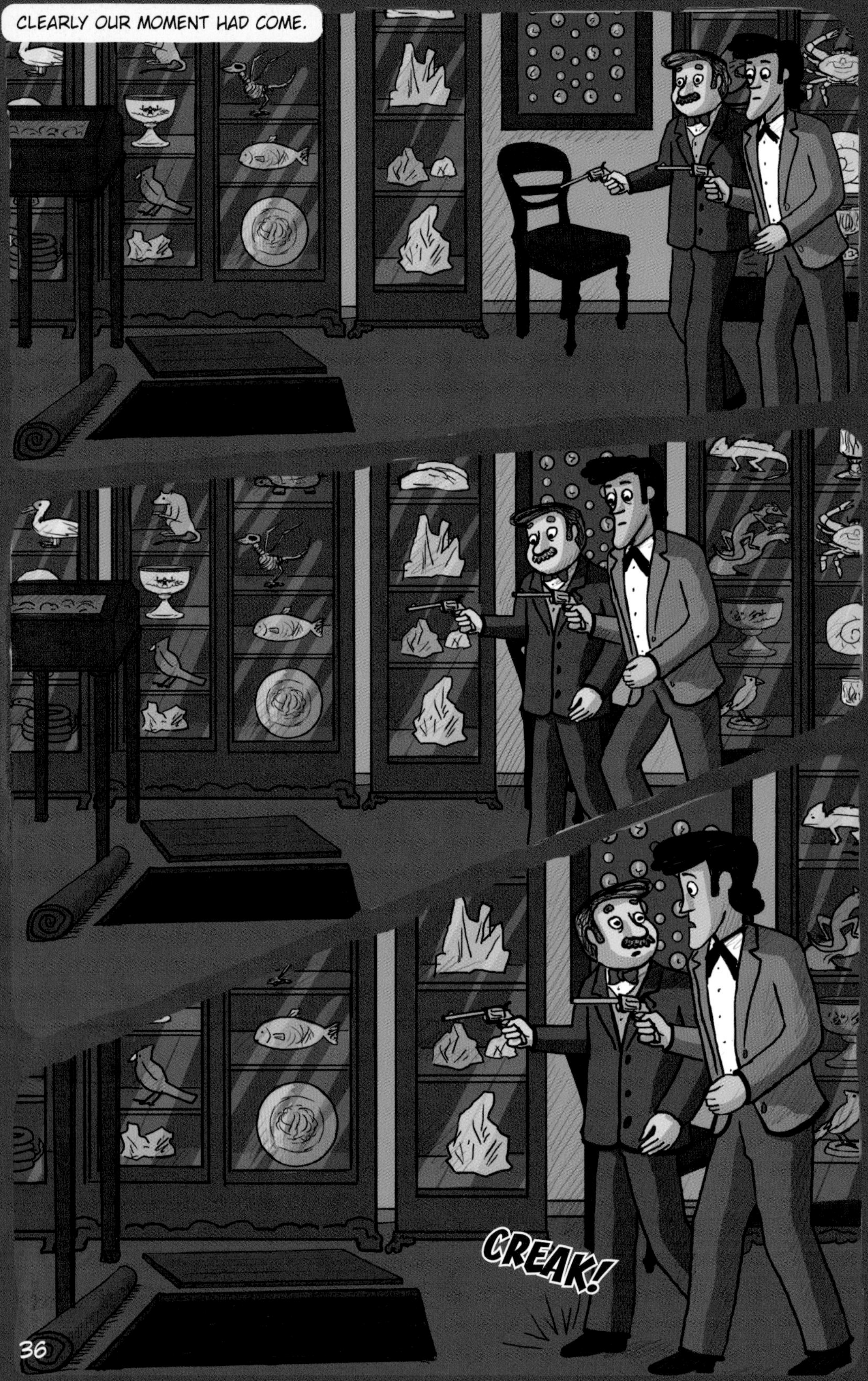
CLEARLY OUR MOMENT HAD COME.
CREAK!

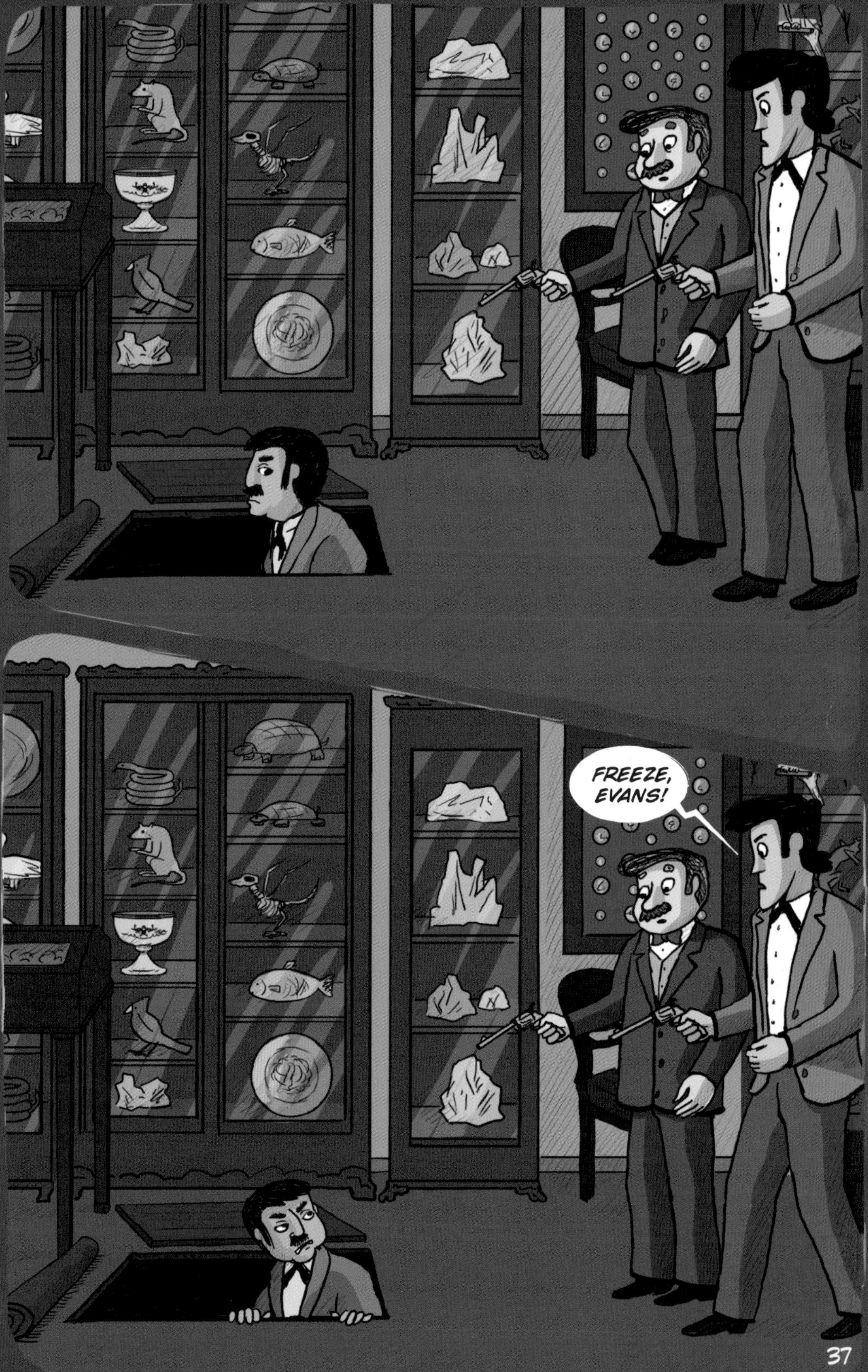
FREEZE, EVANS!

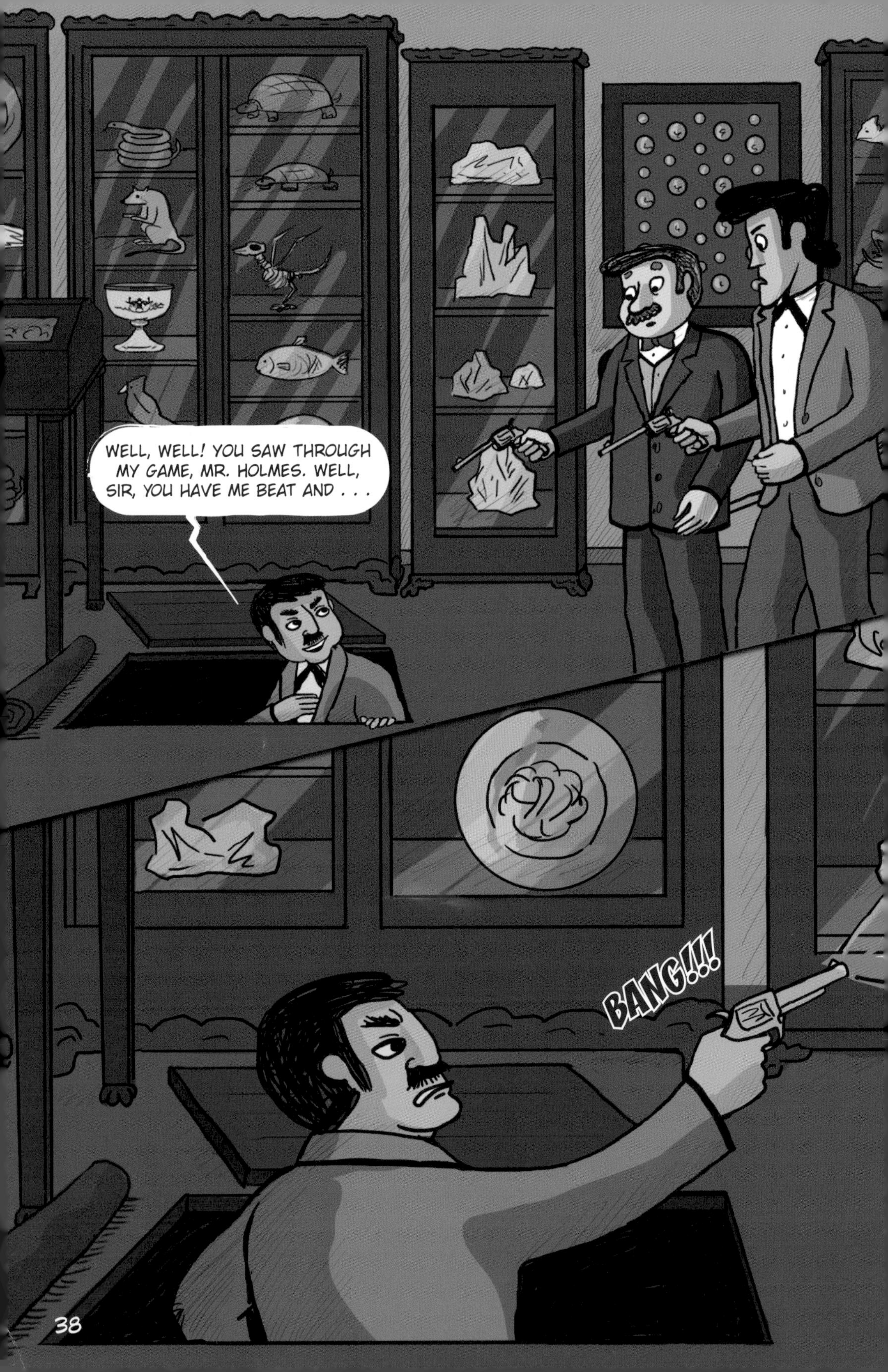
WELL, WELL! YOU SAW THROUGH MY GAME, MR. HOLMES. WELL, SIR, YOU HAVE ME BEAT AND . . .
BANG!!!

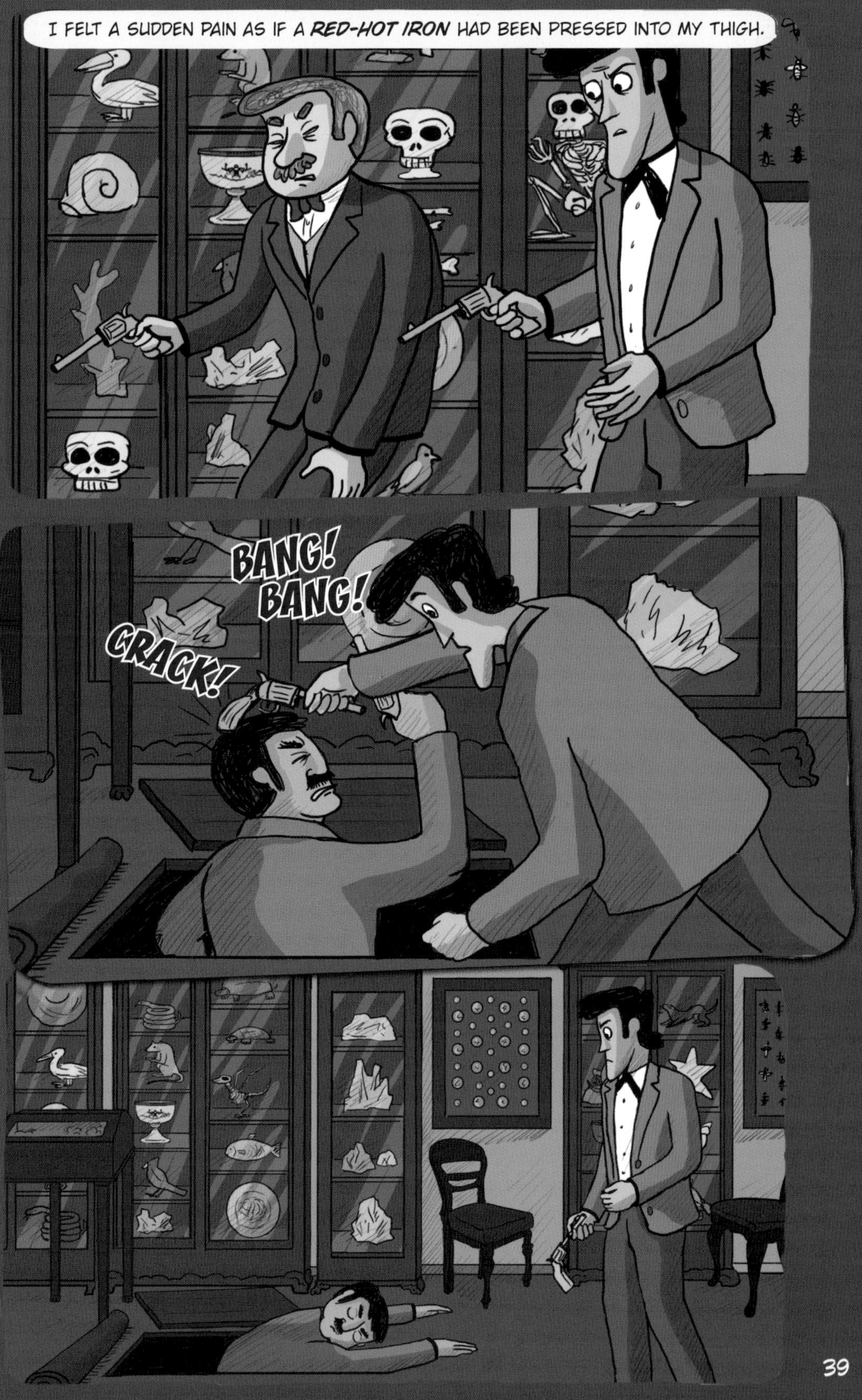
I FELT A SUDDEN PAIN AS IF A RED-HOT IRON HAD BEEN PRESSED INTO MY THIGH.
BANG!
BANG!
CRACK!

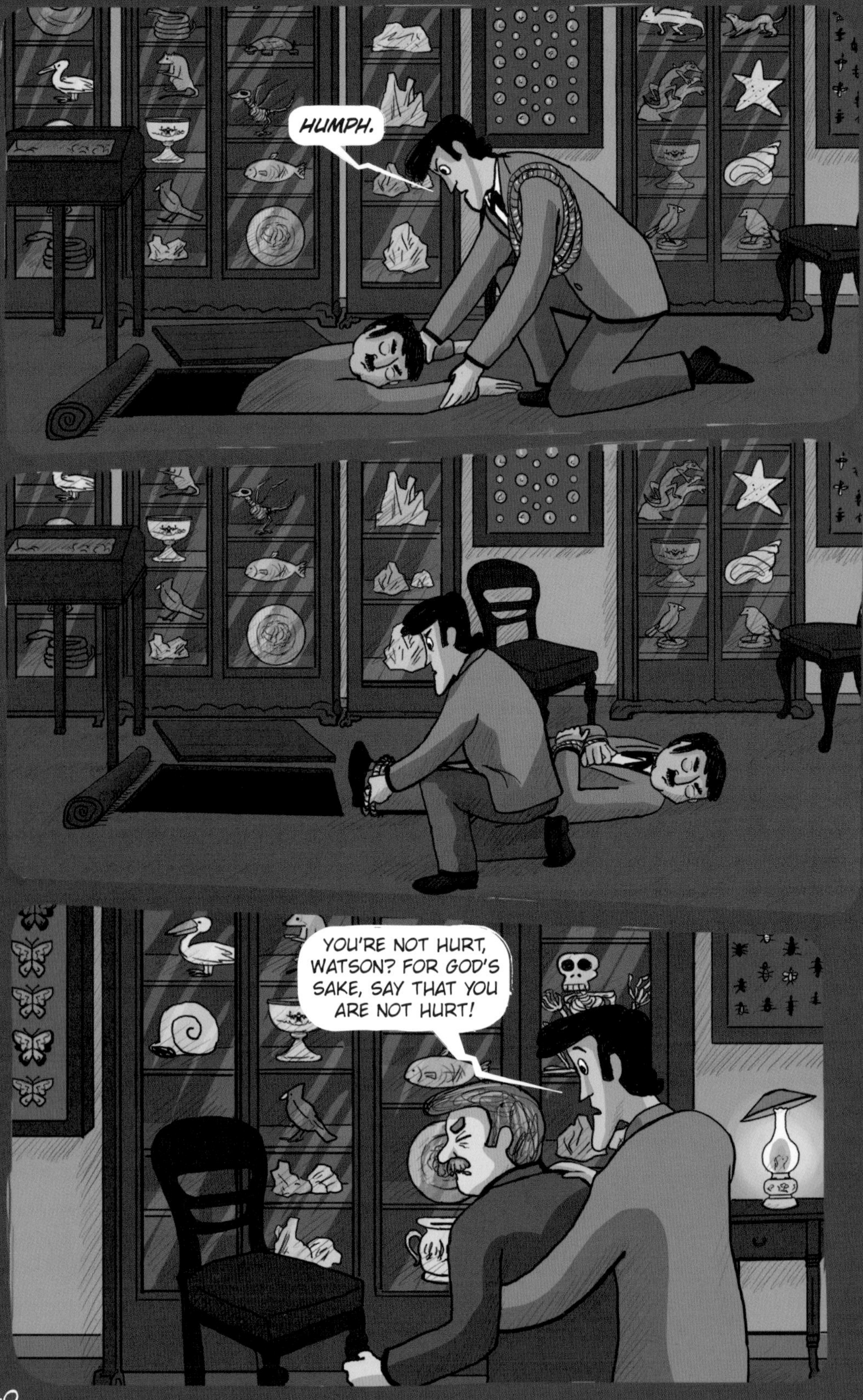
HUMPH.
YOU'RE NOT HURT, WATSON? FOR GOD'S SAKE, SAY THAT YOU ARE NOT HURT!

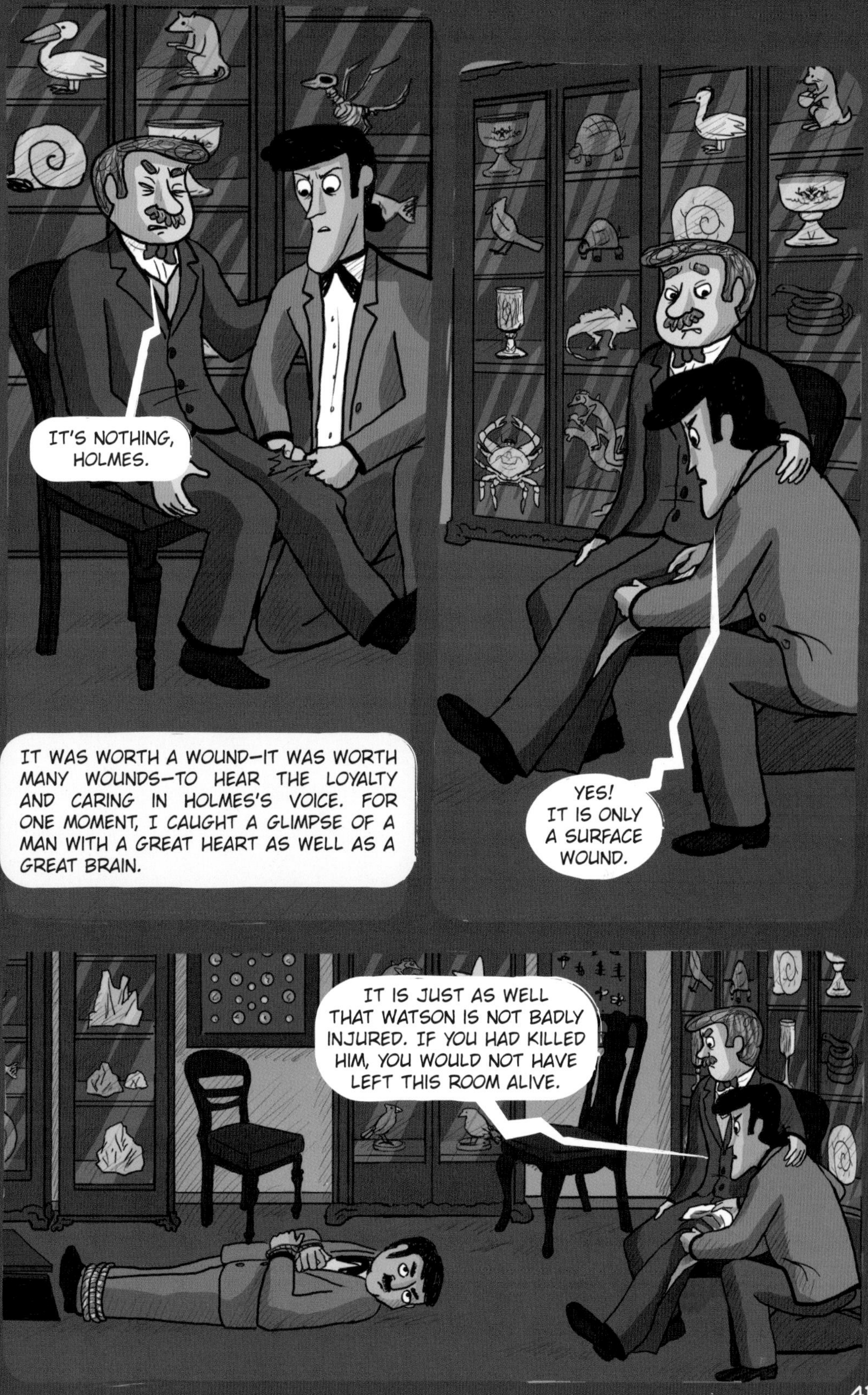
IT'S NOTHING, HOLMES.
IT WAS WORTH A WOUND—IT WAS WORTH MANY WOUNDS—TO HEAR THE LOYALTY AND CARING IN HOLMES'S VOICE. FOR ONE MOMENT, I CAUGHT A GLIMPSE OF A MAN WITH A GREAT HEART AS WELL AS A GREAT BRAIN.
YES! IT IS ONLY A SURFACE WOUND.
IT IS JUST AS WELL THAT WATSON IS NOT BADLY INJURED. IF YOU HAD KILLED HIM, YOU WOULD NOT HAVE LEFT THIS ROOM ALIVE.

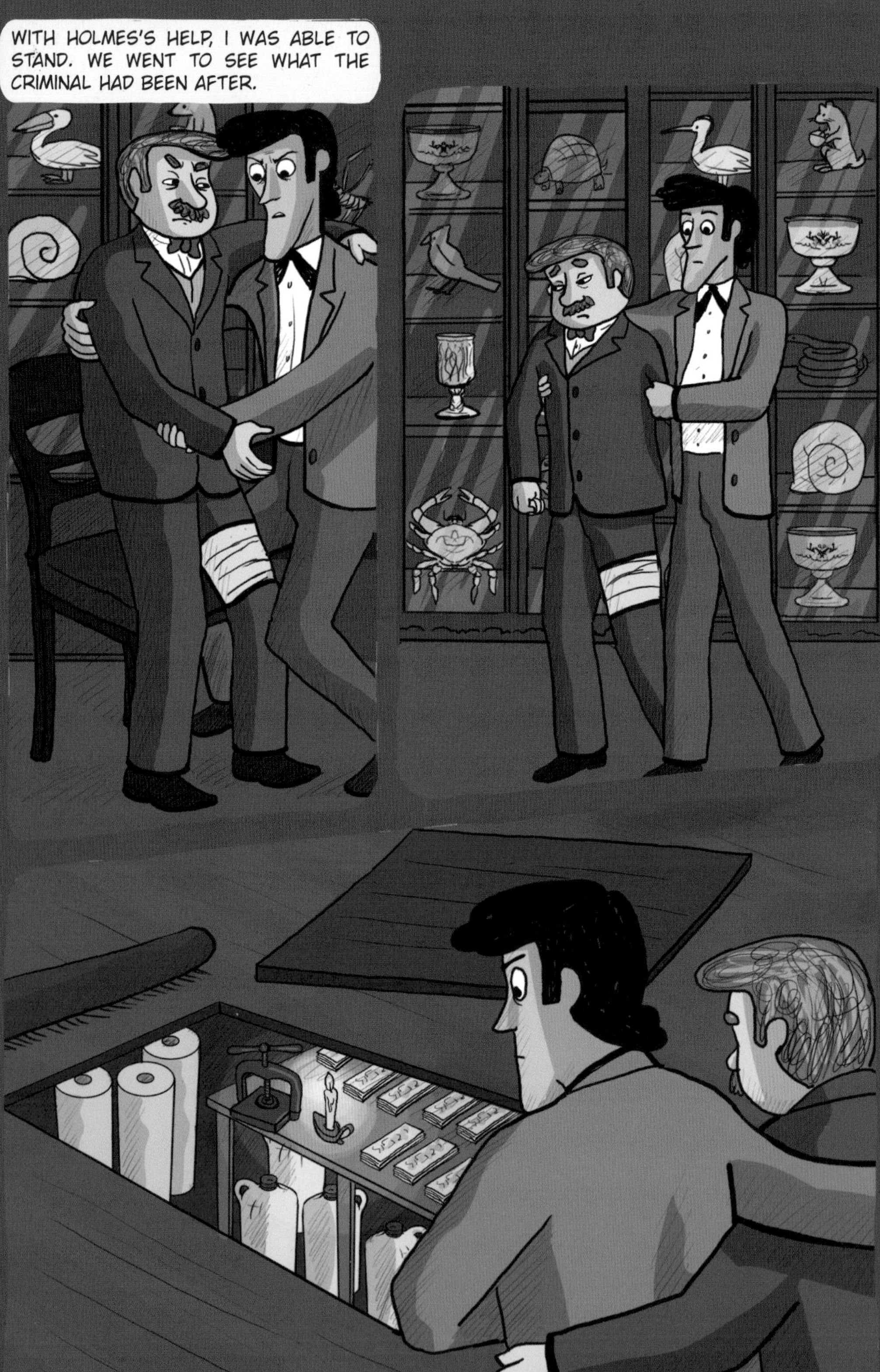
WITH HOLMES'S HELP, I WAS ABLE TO STAND. WE WENT TO SEE WHAT THE CRIMINAL HAD BEEN AFTER.

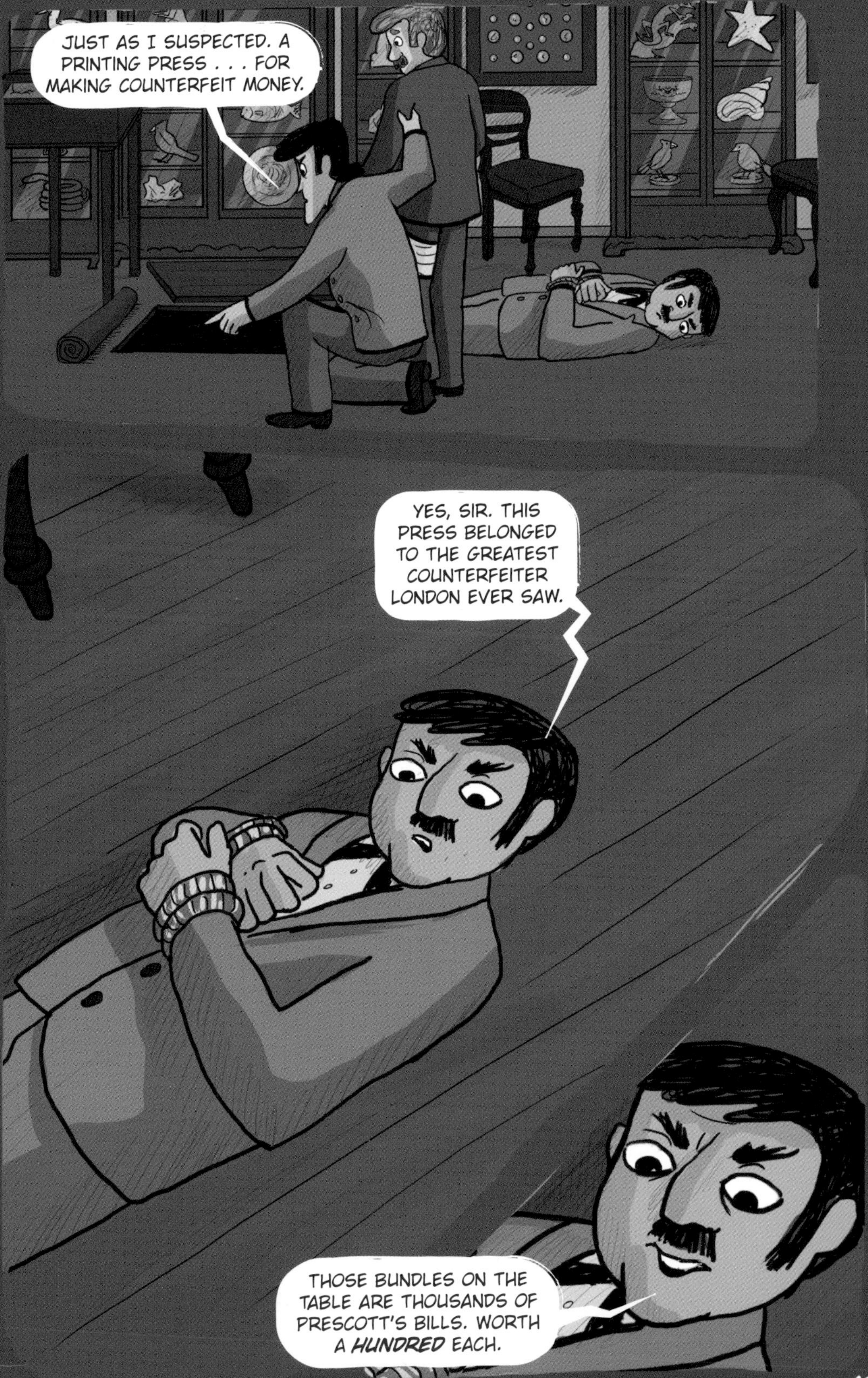
JUST AS I SUSPECTED. A PRINTING PRESS . . . FOR MAKING COUNTERFEIT MONEY.
YES, SIR. THIS PRESS BELONGED TO THE GREATEST COUNTERFEITER LONDON EVER SAW.
THOSE BUNDLES ON THE TABLE ARE THOUSANDS OF PRESCOTT'S BILLS. WORTH A *HUNDRED* EACH.

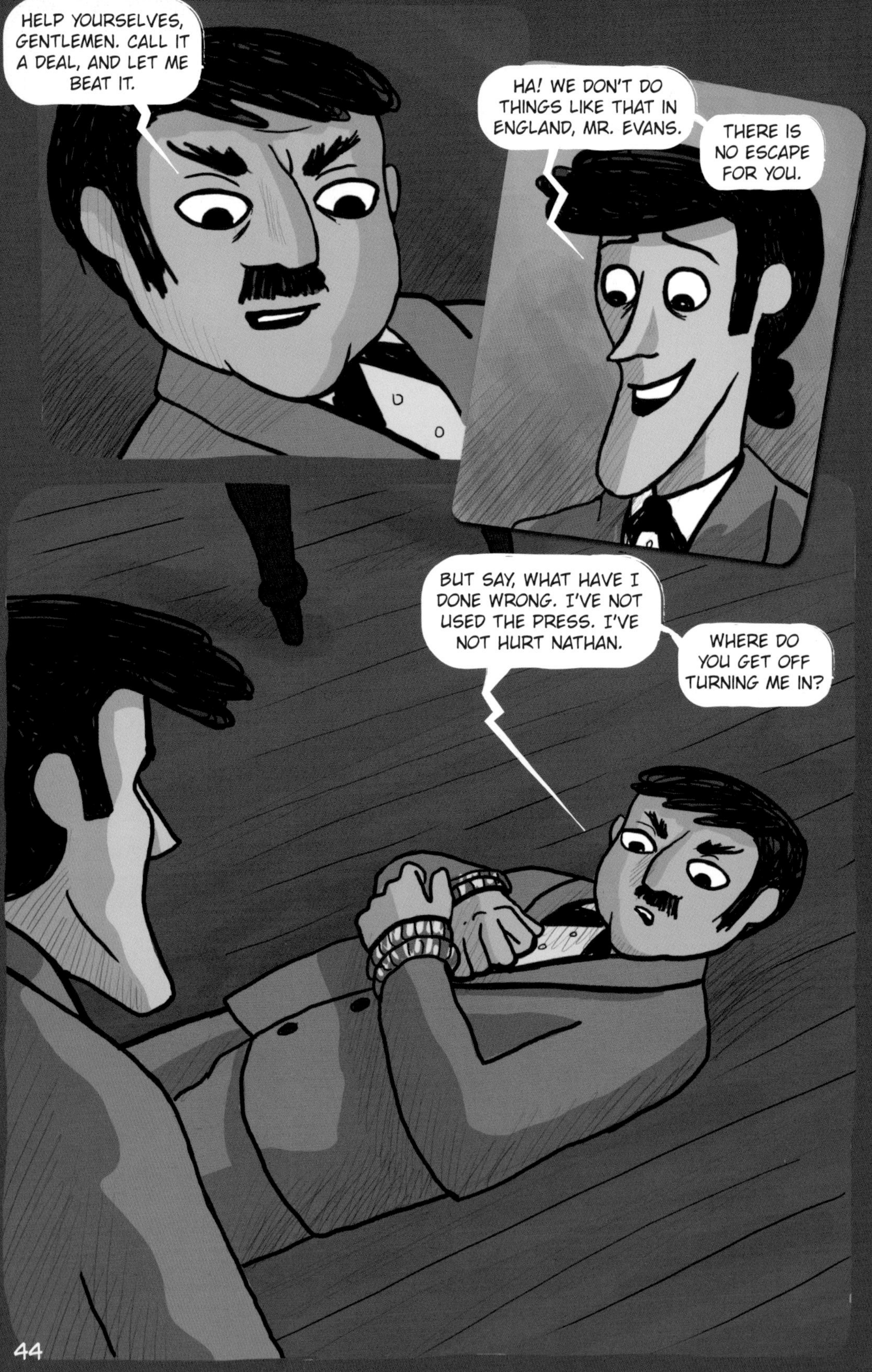
HELP YOURSELVES, GENTLEMEN. CALL IT A DEAL, AND LET ME BEAT IT.
HA! WE DON'T DO THINGS LIKE THAT IN ENGLAND, MR. EVANS.
THERE IS NO ESCAPE FOR YOU.
BUT SAY, WHAT HAVE I DONE WRONG. I'VE NOT USED THE PRESS. I'VE NOT HURT NATHAN.
WHERE DO YOU GET OFF TURNING ME IN?

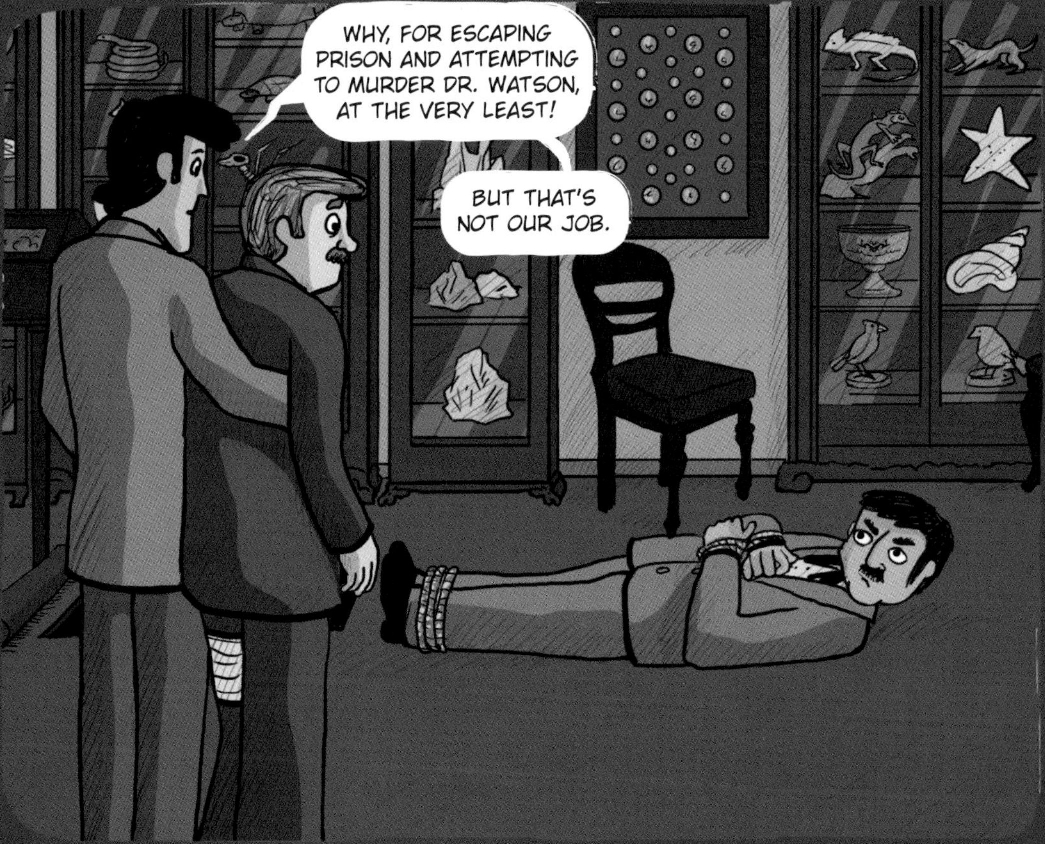
WHY, FOR ESCAPING PRISON AND ATTEMPTING TO MURDER DR. WATSON, AT THE VERY LEAST!
BUT THAT'S NOT OUR JOB.

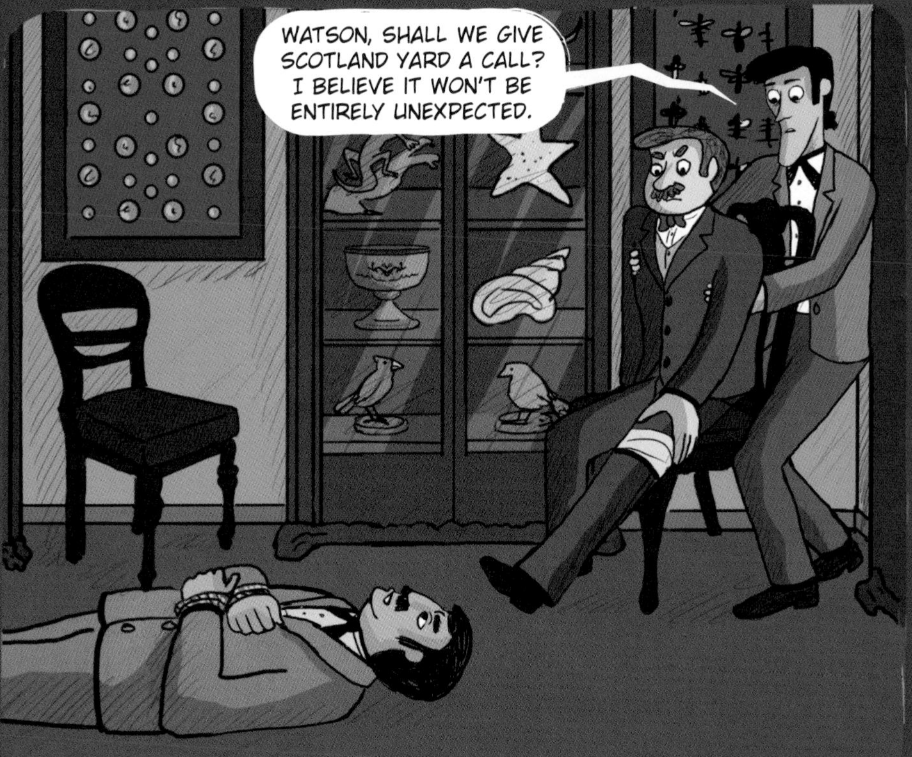
WATSON, SHALL WE GIVE SCOTLAND YARD A CALL? I BELIEVE IT WON'T BE ENTIRELY UNEXPECTED.

From the Desk of
John H. Watson, M.D.

The Adventure of the Three Garridebs: How Did Holmes Solve It?

What was it about John Garrideb that made Holmes suspicious?

John Garrideb claimed to have just arrived in England from America. Yet Holmes noticed that the style and cut of the man's clothes were definitely British. When Holmes suggested that the American had been in England for some time, John Garrideb was eager to change the subject.

How was Holmes able to ascertain that John Garrideb was lying?

Holmes set a trap for the unsuspecting American when he made up his friend, Dr. Starr of Topeka, Kansas. When the man claimed to remember Starr, Holmes was certain that John Garrideb was not telling the truth. Holmes suspected the story of the three Garridebs was a lie as well, but he needed more clues to discover why the American had made up the strange tale.

How did Holmes know that Nathan Garrideb was innocent?

The brass nameplate at Nathan Garrideb's home had begun to discolor with age. Holmes concluded that Nathan Garrideb was not a fake, since his nameplate had been up for several years.

How did Holmes know that Nathan Garrideb's home held what the American wanted?

Holmes knew that Nathan Garrideb's trip to Birmingham was a wild-goose chase, because the advertisement was a fake. Since the older Garrideb never left his room, Holmes suspected that Garrideb's home must hold the key to the mystery. Nathan Garrideb had lived in his room since the previous tenant disappeared in 1895— the same year that a well-known counterfeiter, Roger Prescott, was murdered by the American criminal known as Killer Evans. Holmes guessed that Garrideb's room may once have been the headquarters of a counterfeit money operation.

Once Holmes learned John Garrideb's true identity, how was he able to piece together the mystery?

When Killer Evans, alias John Garrideb, headed straight for the trapdoor in the floor of Nathan Garrideb's home, Holmes's suspicions were confirmed. Roger Prescott must have shown the trapdoor to Killer Evans before he died. Holmes's discovery of the printing press and the thousands of fake bills solved the mystery of the three Garridebs.

Further Reading and Websites

Cosson, M. J. *The Mystery of the Too Crisp Cash.* Logan, IA: Perfection Learning, 1998.

Doyle, Sir Arthur Conan. *The Adventures and the Memoirs of Sherlock Holmes.* New York: Sterling, 2004.

Mason, Paul. *Frauds and Counterfeits.* Mankato, MN: Black Rabbit Books, 2010.

Shearer, Alex. *Canned.* New York: Scholastic, 2008.

Sherlock Holmes Museum
http://www.sherlock-holmes.co.uk

Sir Arthur Conan Doyle Society
http://www.ash-tree.bc.ca/acdsocy.html

Springer, Nancy. *The Case of the Bizarre Bouquets: An Enola Holmes Mystery.* New York: Penguin, 2009.

221 Baker Street
http://221bakerstreet.org

About the Author

Sir Arthur Conan Doyle was born on May 22, 1859. He became a doctor in 1882. When this career did not prove successful, Doyle started writing stories. In addition to the popular Sherlock Holmes short stories and novels, Doyle also wrote historical novels, romances, and plays.

About the Adapters

Murray Shaw's lifelong passion for Sherlock Holmes began when he was a child. He was the author of the Match Wits with Sherlock Holmes series published in the 1990s. For decades, he was a popular speaker in public schools and libraries on the adventures of Holmes and Watson.

M. J. Cosson is the author of more than fifty books, both fiction and nonfiction, for children and young adults. She has long been a fan of mysteries and especially of the great detective, Sherlock Holmes. In fact, she has participated in the production of several Sherlock Holmes plays. A native of Iowa, Cosson lives in the Texas Hill Country with her husband, dogs, and cat.

About the Illustrators

French artist Sophie Rohrbach began her career after graduating in display design at the Chambre des Commerce. She went on to design displays in many top department stores including Galerias Lafayette. She also studied illustration at Emile Cohl school in Lyon, France, where she now lives with her daughter. Rohrbach has illustrated many children's books. She is passionate about the colors and patterns that she uses in her illustrations.

JT Morrow has worked as a freelance illustrator for over twenty years and has won several awards. He specializes in doing parodies and imitations of the Old and Modern Masters—everyone from da Vinci to Picasso. JT also exhibits his paintings at galleries near his home. He lives just south of San Francisco with his wife and daughter.